Animal Crackers

Animal Crackers

Hannah Tinti

LARGE PRINT

This large print edition published in 2004 by
RB Large Print
A division of Recorded Books
A Haights Cross Communications Company
270 Skipjack Road
Prince Frederick, MD 20678

Published by arrangement with Bantam Dell Publishing Group

The following stories appeared in different form in the following publications:

"Animal Crackers" in *Alaska Quarterly Review*, "Home Sweet Home" in *Epoch* and *Best American Mystery Stories 2003*, "Reasonable Terms" in *Story*, "Slim's Last Ride" in *Sonora Review*, "Hit Man of the Year" in *Story*, "Gallus, Gallus" in *Story Quarterly*, "How to Revitalize the Snake in Your Life" in *Another Magazine*.

This book is a work of fiction. Names, characters, places and incidents either are products of the author's imagination or are used fictitiously. Any resemblance to actual events or locales or persons, living or dead, is entirely coincidental.

Publisher's Cataloging In Publication Data
(Prepared by Donohue Group, Inc.)

Tinti, Hannah.
   Animal crackers / Hannah Tinti.

     p. (large print) ; cm.

   ISBN: 1-4193-0496-8

1. Human–animal relationships—Fiction. 2. Animals—Fiction. 3. Large type books. I. Title.

PS3620.I56 A83 2004b
813/.6

Printed in the United States of America

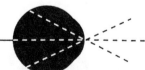

**This Large Print Book carries the
Seal of Approval of N.A.V.H.**

This book is for my parents,
Hester and William Tinti

CONTENTS

ANIMAL CRACKERS

It's time to wash the elephant. Joseph has dragged out the hoses and I'm trying to prod Marysue out the door to the place we do it. Hup, I say, and poke her with a broom. I need to be careful—there is a part of me that steps into traffic—she eased her weight onto the last keeper's foot and the bones were crushed to pieces. I imagine my ex-wife lifting that giant ear and whispering, Step there.

When I started, the staff treated me to a beer and showed me their scars. They said it would happen sooner or later. They said watch out. Everyone who works with animals has a mark somewhere.

Joseph says big animals are like big problems. He should know, he's had his share—eighteen years old when the army shipped him to Cambodia. He came back okay, he says, only to get his arm chomped off by a Senegalese lion in a traveling circus. He's got a little stump coming from the end of his elbow that bends up and down. Like me, Joseph used to have a wife who isn't in the picture anymore. She left him for a soldier who'd also been in Cambodia. Joseph says it was his fault. He doesn't blame the lion.

It's a warm day and I'm sweating in my coveralls. We scrub Marysue's legs and Joseph tells me another story, this one about his friend Al he met in the service (not the one who drove off into the sunset with his wife). I listen to him describe the jungle and turn my hose on the ground to make some mud. Marysue likes to roll in it. She scoops some up, throws it across her back, and I take a long-handled brush and rub it in. She looks at me with her mouth open and I think she is saying thanks.

Joseph's friend Al was stationed near Phnom Penh and had a pet cockatoo he'd bought off the street for a buck. It would sit on his shoulder and squawk, feathers rippling, but mostly it just looked around and moved its feet back and forth. Al taught it to shit on command. He'd make it go on his friends as a joke, or on people he didn't like, for a different kind of joke.

One day they were at a bar with the cockatoo flying around and it suddenly landed on Al's shoulder and let loose some of its sparkling white fruit. It had never done this before—Joseph laughed—but Al just sat and stared at it spackling down the camouflage green of his army jacket. He said, I'm going to die, and he did—somebody had booby-trapped his bike and it blew when he turned the ignition. Joseph said he saw the cockatoo flying around after that, looking for its master, and finally

4

Joseph got so mad he knocked it out of a tree and broke its neck. He still had both his arms then.

I watch Joseph to see how he's feeling, but he doesn't seem angry anymore. He slides a sponge across Marysue's feet and says that manatees have the same kind of rounded nails on their flippers. He says they're the closest thing elephants have to a relative. I try to imagine Marysue floating in the water, suddenly free of all that weight. Elephants can swim for miles, Joseph says. Somehow they know they're not going to sink.

Sandy runs the monkey house. She is an attractive woman if you look at her from the left. When she turns, you can see the puckered skin and the crooked white line across her cheek into her chin where a gorilla took a bite out. The scar just touches the corner of her mouth, so when she smiles, the skin stretches and it looks like something's still holding on to her.

She studied biology and zoology in college. After graduation she got hired by one of her professors as a research assistant and headed into the African jungle. She was thinking she had the touch, and it made her do things she shouldn't, like get too close to a newborn gorilla and have the mother come charging out of the bushes and bury her teeth in Sandy's face until the team they were traveling with shot her down. Sandy woke up in a hospital to doctors clicking their tongues

5

as they sewed her skin back together over the bone.

We went out on a date once. I took her to dinner and a movie and we got a drink afterward. She told me her old boyfriend used to make her keep her head turned when they made love, so he wouldn't have to look at it. Hearing all this made me uneasy, the way people can tell you secrets about themselves too soon and make you feel responsible. I took her home after that and left as soon as I could.

Mike takes care of the sea lions, George and Martha. He has a master's degree in poetry and has worked here, scrubbing the tank, for seven years. Each day at noon he performs a show, throwing fish from a pail to George and Martha as they bob on the surface of the water. Afterward, if the boss isn't around, he tries to sell copies of his chapbook to the crowd.

One evening after we split a bottle of schnapps, our pants rolled up and our feet in the sea lion pool, Mike told me about how he went diving at night off the coast of Mexico with a few of his buddies. He said jumping into the ocean after dark is like stepping down into a graveyard, falling through the earth, bumping into coffins and bodies, and feeling all of the lost bits and pieces of souls that have seeped into the soil come looking for you. He said he'd never do it again.

The men brought underwater lights to look at things. They attached glow sticks to their tanks, each a different color—green, yellow, purple. They held on to their masks and regulators and fell in backward.

The group went down about eighty feet and let the current take them. Bugs swarmed their flashlights, and Mike could feel little insects wiggling against him as they got caught in his wet suit. He saw giant lobsters, jellyfish, skates, sharks, and other strange things he didn't know the names for, creatures that only come out at night.

Mike swept the light below. Just beyond the beam was an enormous scaly movement that didn't seem to end—part of a manta wing, or the curve of a tail. The animal churned steadily beneath him and there were things hanging—spines or leeches—bits of detritus in its wake. Mike willed himself not to panic. He turned off his light, as if caught spying on his neighbors, and paused in the stillness of the water. Then he swam as fast as he could.

He stopped at thirty feet for safety, to keep from getting the bends. He clicked on the flashlight and looked behind him. There was a tiny eel. A school of fish. Mike watched the green glow of a light stick slowly moving toward him and felt a gathering of relief. Together he and his friend treaded water, back and forth, while they waited for their buddy to join them. They could see the purple color of him in the distance.

When he didn't come any closer, they got nervous and went after him. He wasn't there. It was only his tanks settled on the ocean floor, the glow stick swaying like a weather vane in the direction of a bad wind. They went back to the boat, but he wasn't there either and by then they were out of reserve. They radioed for help. Mike used a snorkel and his flashlight to keep looking, but he stayed close to the boat. They never found the body.

Mike threw the empty schnapps bottle into the pool. We were both quiet for a while. I had my fingers wrapped around the railing and I thought about all the little kids who would be pressing their faces against the glass tomorrow. We had some more quiet between us and then he waded in to fish it out.

You hear animal stories every day. How a bee stung little Johnny and he went into cardiac arrest. How a snake bit Cousin Tom and it shriveled up his toe. How a pack of dogs chased Aunt Shirley down the street until she climbed through an open car window, rolled it shut behind her, and watched the animals circling, pawing the doors, their wet noses leaving streaks on the chrome. These stories are supposed to give warning.

Joseph scrapes away at the bottom of Marysue's foot. He touches her below the knee and she lifts her leg automatically, as if his fingers are telling her something important. I know not to make any sudden movements now. She watched me as if I might attack, because this is when another animal would come, when she is not ready to protect

8

herself. Her eyes seem too small for such a large body. She keeps her trunk on Joseph's back, feeling around, making sure of what is happening to her.

Joseph says that in the wild when elephants feel threatened, they put the young and the weak in the middle and form a circle around them. I wonder if Marysue had family somewhere. If they tried to save her from being tagged and shipped. I picture her searching for a tail to hold on to while the others paw the ground and get ready to charge.

Ann runs the ticket booth. Her cat, Stinky, comes to work with her every day. Ann keeps a small basket by her feet, where he sleeps. Stinky doesn't have any fur. His skin hangs down between his legs like an old man wearing a diaper. Ann says Stinky saved her life.

She tells me about one night in September when she woke up to a blazing light in her room. Her bed was vibrating and she thought it was an earthquake until she felt her body rise and start to move toward the window. The sash flew up and the screen was ripped off. Ann says what came next was like the sting you get before frostbite, followed by a numbness that crept from her fingers and toes and moved through her thighs, her shoulders, and on toward her heart. She tried to scream, but her throat was swollen tight.

Stinky jumped onto the windowsill and started hissing. He had fur then, Ann says, orange and yellow swirled together, and it stood on end, prickling against the beam like needle points. Stinky bared his teeth and Ann says his eyes reflected the light so intensely it looked like lasers shooting out of him, and suddenly everything went dark and Ann dropped to the ground, hitting the back of her head on the bedside table. She clutched the rag rug on the floor around her and crawled underneath the mattress, where she lay stunned until morning. When daylight came and she had enough courage to come out, she found the window still open, shreds of the screen in the bushes outside and Stinky, bald and quivering, under a pile of dirty clothes in the closet.

When she isn't collecting tickets, Ann travels around the country going to abductee conventions with her cat, holding on to his hairless body as truth. She will not go anywhere without him. I watch Stinky through the glass while he is sleeping and I think about devotion. I know Ann worries what will happen when he dies, and why shouldn't she—she knows what it's like to live alone—and when he's gone and the light comes back into her room, she'll know as she's being pulled through the window that this time she is being taken away because there is no one who loves her enough to stop it.

I pick up a bunch of alfalfa and hold it in the air. Marysue reaches with her trunk and takes it out of my hand. As soon as the food is in, she's back to see if I have any more. Her trunk searches my palm as if she is reading my lifeline.

Joseph says that elephants can recognize dead relatives by feeling their bones. They spend hours turning over the remains, stroking the curves of the skull. Sometimes, they will take pieces away with them and carry them for miles before letting them go.

Ike is the owner. I like him fine, as do most of the other people who work here. He's got a story too, and he told it when he interviewed me. Ike asked if I had experience with animals and I told him that I could communicate with dogs. He had a miniature dachshund asleep at his heels and I said, Watch this, and started making groans in the back of my throat. The dog wouldn't even raise his head to look at me. Ike said, You need the job that bad, or are you just plain crazy? I said I needed the job and he said, Okay then.

Ike's part Eskimo. He grew up near the Bering Sea, in Unalakleet, Alaska. Many of the men would work on the oil rigs and be gone for months at a time. This gave the village an abandoned feeling, even with all the women and children around, but it also gave Ike a lot of freedom. He liked to hang with boys who were older. The Iditarod sled dog race came through each year, and when this happened, the kids would go crazy, building ramshackle sleds and hitching up their dogs, who more often than not knocked them over and escaped, dragging pieces of sheet metal behind them for the rest of the day.

To get around this problem, Ike's friend George decided to strap his little brother onto the sled first before tying it to the family dog, a young husky with a habit of running away. The dog took off, dragging George's little brother screaming into the distance, and the two boys had to track them down. They'd gone a mile out and were about to bridge a hill when they found a little blue hat, the kind that ties under your chin. Ike picked it up and they went over the top, and there was a polar bear ripping the guts out of George's little brother. He'd already torn apart the dog—the snow was covered with blood—the sled overturned, the rope hanging loosely from the husky's neck. George started screaming and the bear turned to look, its muzzle wet with red, and that was it—Ike ran.

He got about ten feet away when George passed him. George was older and his legs were flying fast. Ike got this feeling down the back of his neck between his shoulder blades and he knew the bear was coming and it was almost as if he could see the arm reach out and knock him over. Ike's feet fell out from underneath him. He landed on his face, his lips stinging in the snow. He didn't move. He felt the lumbering body of the bear crunching next to him through the powder and he lost it; he pissed all over himself.

Ike heard the nose. It started at his feet and snorted between his legs. It shnuffed and panted over his body and sounded like a person getting ready to tell a secret as it moved closer to his ear. He felt the warmth of the bear's breath and closed his eyes. There was snow on his wrists between his mittens and his jacket, and he thought about the skin there, how it got red and itched by the fire while his mom cooked him oatmeal and when she wasn't feeling lonely played the spoons, rattling the backs of the silverware against her knee, then down between her fingers, until she got a rhythm together and she could sing. The nose was at his crotch again. He listened to the bear walk away.

He stayed there in the snow for a long time. When he raised his head, it was dusk. In the distance he saw a snowmobile coming, but he couldn't bring himself to move. Ike tells me sometimes you have these experiences, and you spend the rest of your life thinking about them. Try to shut out what happened and it comes back stronger, a nagging unease, an unanswerable question, and you have to go through it all over again.

Marysue likes it when I pet her tongue. It is a large and frightening muscle, and as I rub my hand across it I try not to think about her swallowing my arm. I use my left, thinking that I would not miss it as much as my right. I take the hose and start a final rinse down her side. The coarse black hairs growing out from between the wrinkles in her skin hang dripping with the weight of the water. I think of these hairs later that night when I am home safe and sound and stepping out of a hot shower, having washed all the animal smells off from the day. I run the towel underneath my arms, across my chest, and down each of my legs. When I reach my toes, I dry thoroughly between them and think about my ex-wife again. *Step there.*

I met her in a bar in Las Vegas. She was in for a convention, a gathering of nurses who'd worked in mobile hospitals during Vietnam. I was pouring drinks. She told me a story about how she saved a guy's life in a restaurant with a steak knife and a ballpoint pen, performing a tracheotomy between courses. I watched her throat as she drank her martini, the way the glands clutched and moved along her neck. Cutting him was instinctive, she said, and I leaned across the bar and kissed her.

We had a drive-through wedding. Rented a convertible for the day and packed a picnic. She wore a white baseball cap with a veil stapled to the back. Afterward we drove over the Hoover Dam and she stood and hollered as we crossed, her dress flying up around her waist, her lipstick worn off. She'd been divorced already, once. I used to kid her about it on our long-distance phone calls when we first started dating, but when I convinced her to move in—to leave her job and start over—she made me promise not to mention it again. I don't want to be reminded of anything, she said, and I told her that's why people got married.

Our daughter's name is Leigh Ann. She was born with Down syndrome, and even though my wife didn't say it, I could tell by the way she sniffed that she suspected my Midwestern genes. When she left me, she took Leigh Ann to her parents in New Mexico, where I would drive every weekend, spending awkward hours on their front porch with my baby in my lap. I put up in a motel nearby, and Monday morning I'd drive back to Las Vegas, the desert reaching out around me in every direction as if I were the center of something great. It used to make me feel like screaming, and sometimes I did, the windows down and the air rushing into my mouth.

She called the bar to let me know she was moving in with her boyfriend and taking Leigh Ann with her. I had a law school student who worked with me, paying loans with tips, get on the phone and tell her she had to let me know where they were going. She gave him an address, which turned out to be bogus, and I got on the highway to her parents' house. They wouldn't tell me where she was. They said I didn't deserve to know.

The year after we were married, we had an apartment in Carson City. It was on the third floor, a railroad, one long hallway with a window at the end that opened onto a fire escape. Warm summer nights after I got off work, I would jump from the street to catch hold of the iron railing, pull myself up, and climb to our place. I thought it was romantic.

One night I got to the bar and they'd scheduled two of us by mistake. Maggie, a girl from the Philippines who was into astronomy, was already pouring. She told me that Mars was supposed to be out that night and how to look for it. She told me it had a radius of 2,110 miles and that it took 687 days to go around the sun. Once I got home, I stood outside our building and found it, a tiny red flickering light in the sky. It made me wonder how many other stars and planets were out there just beyond that I couldn't see, and how that didn't make them any less real.

I climbed the fire escape and found the window locked and the lights out in our apartment. I started banging on the frame, and just when I thought I was going to have to go back down, I saw the door at the end of the apartment open, and the light from the hall showed a man leaving.

My wife came to the window in a bathrobe. Her smile was weak as she turned the lock. She opened the sash and said, Aren't you going to come in, and I reached out and touched her cheek and then slammed her head into the windowsill, and that is the first time I hurt her that night. I pushed her back into the room and she fell on the floor and knocked over a table and a lamp and that was the second time I hurt her. The third time was when I grabbed her by the hair and dragged her down the hallway to the kitchen. The fourth happened when I kicked her. The fifth, sixth, seventh, eighth, and ninth came as I slapped her, my palm itching. I thought of a knife, but I took the blender sitting on the counter instead and I threw it, and that was the last time I hurt her. It knocked her out. Her

16

nose was broken and there was blood seeping into the terry cloth. I leaned against the wall to catch my breath. Leigh Ann was crying in the bedroom.

I sat down at our kitchen table—the table where we ate English muffins and spread jelly—looked at my trembling fingers, and realized that I was happy. Later, after the bruises were gone and she left me, I sat in the same place and touched my skin, my muscles aching as if my body had been pulled into pieces and hastily patched back together, but in that moment I knew that I had touched something raw and wonderful that resonated in my bones, and it wasn't until I heard the cries of my daughter that I came back to that apartment, that room, and that life which was before me and I told myself, You have a child, you have to take care.

I've heard stories about elephants that go crazy. I look at Marysue and wonder if she's got it in her. I take the broom I use to guide her back to her cage and poke it hard under her ribs. She lets out a puff and then a groan and I know it hurt. She turns and gives me a look with her eye. I rub my hand up and down her back leg to make up and she lets loose a pile of shit, her tail lifting slightly to one side.

Joseph starts picking up the hoses with his arm, coiling them around his shoulder and holding them in place with the stump he has left. He says I think too much. He says, Why don't you work somewhere else. Then he looks sorry and says he's not trying to get rid of me. I wonder then if he knows, but he goes home the same time as usual and leaves me to do the final cleanup. I muck out the stall and spread down fresh hay for the night.

When I'm done I take off my shoes, lay my body on the floor of Marysue's cage, touch her under the knee like Joseph, and put my head under her foot. She lets the bottom rest on my ear, the cement chilling my cheek, the smell like the damp fertility of dirt under rocks. She shifts her weight and my head rolls gently back and forth. I can hear her breathing. It echoes off the walls and sounds piped in, a recording of an elephant still living in the wild. I close my eyes, imagine banyan trees, and feel a heaviness lift.

HOME SWEET HOME

Pat and Clyde were murdered on pot roast night. The doorbell rang just as Pat was setting the butter and margarine (Clyde was watching his cholesterol) on the table. She was thinking about James Dean. Pat had loved him desperately as a teenager, seen his movies dozens of times, written his name across her notebooks, carefully taped pictures of him to the inside of her locker so that she would have the pleasure of seeing his tortured, sullen face from East of Eden as she exchanged her French and English textbooks for science and math. When she graduated from high school, she took down the photos and pasted them to the inside cover of her yearbook, which she perused longingly several times over the summer and brought with her to the University of Massachusetts, where it sat, unopened, alongside her thesaurus and abridged collegiate dictionary until she met Clyde, received her M.R.S. degree, and packed her things to move into their two-bedroom ranch house on Bridge Street.

Before she put the meat in the oven that afternoon, Pat had made herself a cup of tea and turned on the television. Channel 56 was showing *Rebel without a Cause,* and as the light slowly began to rise through the screen of their old Zenith, she saw James Dean on the steps of the planetarium, clutching at the mismatched socks of a dead Sal Mineo and crying. She put down her tea, slid her warm fingertips inside the V neck of her dress, and held her left breast. Her heart was suddenly pounding, her nipple hard and erect against the palm of her hand. It was like seeing an old lover, like remembering a piece of herself that no longer existed. She watched the credits roll and glanced outside to see her husband mowing their lawn. He had a worried expression on his face and his socks pulled up to his knees.

That evening before dinner, as she arranged the butter and margarine side by side on the table—one yellow airy and light, the other hard and dark like the yolk of an egg—she wondered how she could have forgotten the way James Dean's eyebrows curved. *Isn't memory a strange thing,* she thought. *I could forget all of this, how everything feels, what all of these things mean to me.* She was suddenly seized with the desire to grab the sticks of butter and margarine in her hands and squeeze them until her fingers went right through, to somehow imprint their textures and colors on her brain like a stamp, to make them something that she would never lose. And then she heard the bell.

When she opened the door, Pat noticed that it was still daylight. The sky was blue and bright and clear and she had a fleeting, guilty thought that she should not have spent so much time indoors. After that she crumpled backward into the hall as the bullet from a .38-caliber Saturday Night Special pierced her chest, exited below her shoulder blade, and jammed into the wood of the stairs, where it would later be dug out with a pen knife by Lieutenant Sales and dropped gingerly into a transparent plastic baggie.

Pat's husband, Clyde, was found in the kitchen by the back door, a knife in his hand (first considered a defense against his attacker and later determined to be the carver of the roast). He had been shot twice—once in the stomach and once in the head—and then covered with cereal, the boxes lined up on the counter beside him and the crispy golden contents of Cap'n Crunch, cornflakes, and Special K emptied out over what remained of his face.

Nothing had been stolen.

It was a warm spring evening full of summer promises. Pat and Clyde's bodies lay silent and still while the orange sunset crossed the floors of their house and the streetlights clicked on. As darkness came and the skunks waddled through the backyard and the raccoons crawled down from the trees, they were still there, holding their places, suspended in a moment of quiet blue before the sun came up and a new day started and life went on without them.

It was Clyde's mother who called the police. She

dialed her son's number every Sunday morning from Rhode Island. These phone calls always somehow perfectly coincided with breakfast, or whenever Pat and Clyde were on the verge of making love.

Thar she blows, Clyde would say, and take his hot coffee with him over to where the phone hung on the wall, or slide out of bed with an apologetic glance at his wife. The coffee and Pat would inevitably cool, and in this way his mother would ruin every Sunday. It had been years now since they had frolicked in the morning, but once, when they were first married and Pat was preparing breakfast, she had heard the phone, walked over to where her husband was reading the paper, dropped to her knees, pulled open his robe, and taken him in her mouth. *Let it ring,* she thought, and he had let it ring. Fifteen minutes later the police were on their front porch with smiles as Clyde, red-faced, bathrobe bulging, answered their questions at the door.

In most areas of her life Clyde's mother was a very nice person. She behaved in such a kind and decorous manner that people would often remark, having met her, *What a lovely woman.* But with Clyde she lost her head. She was suspicious, accusing, and tyrannical. After her husband died, she became even worse. Once she got through her grief, her son became her man. She pushed this sense of responsibility through him like fishhooks, plucking on the line, reeling him back in when

24

she felt her hold slipping, so that the points became embedded in his flesh so deep that it would kill him to take them out.

She dialed the police after trying her son thirty-two times, and because the lieutenant on duty was a soft touch, his own mother having recently passed, a cruiser was dispatched to Pat and Clyde's on Bridge Street, and because one of the policemen was looking to buy in the neighborhood, the officers decided to check out the back of the house after they got no answer, and because there was cereal blowing around in the yard, the men got suspicious, and because it was a windy day and because the hinges had recently been oiled and because the door had been left unlocked and swung open and because one of them had seen a dead body before, a suicide up in Hanover, and knew blood and brain and bits of skull when he saw them, he made the call back to the station, because his partner was quietly vomiting in the rosebushes, and said, *We've got trouble.*

Earlier that morning Mrs. Mitchell had let her dog out with a sad, affectionate pat on his behind. Buster was a Labrador retriever and treated all the yards on Bridge Street as if they were his own, making his way leisurely through flower beds, pausing for a drink from a sprinkler, tearing into garbage bags, and relieving himself among patches of newly planted rutabagas. Before long he was digging a hole in Pat and Clyde's backyard.

There were small golden flakes scattered on the grass. Buster licked one up and crunched. The flakes were food, and the dog followed the promise of more across the lawn, through the back door, and over to Clyde, stiff and covered with flies, the remaining cereal a soggy wet pile of pink plaster across his shoulders. The rug underneath the kitchen table was soaked in blood. Buster left red paw prints as he walked around the body and sniffed at the slippers on the dead man's feet. The dog smelled Clyde's last moment, curled into the arch of his foot.

The doorbell had chimed just as Clyde pierced the roast with the carving fork, releasing two streams of juice, which ran down the sides of the meat until they were captured by the raised edge of the serving plate. He paused then as he lifted the knife, waiting to hear and recognize the voices of his wife and whoever had come to visit. His stomach tightened in the silence. He was hungry. When the shot exploded he felt it all at once and everywhere—in the walls, in his eyes, in his chest, in his arms, in the utensils he was holding, in the piece of meat he was carving, in the slippers that placed him on the floor, in the kitchen, before their evening meal.

Buster pulled off one of the slippers and sank his teeth into it. He worked on removing the stuffing of the inner lining and kept his eye on the dead man, who used to shoo-shoo him away from garbage bags, from munching the daffodils that lined the walk, from humping strays behind the garage. Once, after catching the dog relieving himself in the middle of the driveway, Clyde had dragged him by the collar all the way down Bridge Street. *Listen to me, pooch*, Mr. Mitchell had said after Clyde left, one hand smoothing where the collar had choked and the other hand vigorously scratching the dog's behind. *You shit wherever you feel like shitting.*

When the dog decided to leave the house, he took the slipper with him. He dragged it over to the hole he'd already started and threw it in. Buster walked back and forth over the spot once it was filled, then lifted his leg to mark it.

The Mitchells had brought their dog with them when they moved into the neighborhood. Three years later, a son arrived—not a newborn baby decked out in bonnets but a thin, dark boy of indiscriminate age. His name was Miguel, and it was unclear to the people living on Bridge Street whether he was adopted or a child from a previous marriage. He called the Mitchells his mother and father, enrolled in the public school for their district, and quietly became a part of their everyday lives.

In fact, Miguel was the true son of Mr. Mitchell, sired unknowingly on a business trip with a Venezuelan prostitute some seven years before. The mother had been killed in a bus accident along with 53 other travelers on a road outside of

Caracas, and the local police had contacted Mr. Mitchell from a faded company card she had left pressed in her Bible. After a paternity test, the boy arrived at Logan Airport with a worn-out blanket and duffel bag full of chickens (his pets), which were quickly confiscated by customs officials. Mr. Mitchell drove down Route 128 in his station wagon, amazed and panicked at his sudden parenthood, trying to comfort the sobbing boy and wondering how Miguel had managed to keep the birds silent on the plane.

When they pulled into the driveway, Mrs. Mitchell was waiting with a glass of warm milk sweetened with sugar. She was wearing dungarees. She took the boy in her arms and carried him immediately into the bathroom, where she sat him on the counter and washed his face, his hands, his knees, and his feet. Miguel sipped the milk while Mrs. Mitchell gently ran the washcloth behind his ears. When she was finished she tucked him in to their guest bed and read him a stack of Curious George books in Spanish, which she had ordered from their local bookstore. She showed Miguel a picture of the little monkey in the hospital getting a shot from a nurse, and the boy fell asleep, a finger hooked around the belt loop of her jeans. Mrs. Mitchell sat on the bed beside him quietly until he rolled over and let it go.

Mr. Mitchell had met his wife at a gas station in northern California. He had just completed his business degree, and was driving a rented car up the coast to see the Olympic rain forest. She was in a pickup truck with Oregon plates. They both got out and started pumping. Mr. Mitchell finished first, and on his way back to his car after paying, he watched the muscles in her thick arm flexing as she replaced the hose. She glanced up, caught him looking, and smiled. She was not beautiful, but one of her teeth stuck out charmingly sideways. There was a confidence about her, an air of efficiency that made him believe she was the kind of woman who could solve any problem. He started the car, turned out of the station, and glanced into his rearview mirror. He watched the pickup take the opposite road, and as it drove away he felt such a pull that he turned around and followed it for sixty miles.

At the rest stop, he pretended that he was surprised to see her. Later he discovered that many people followed his wife, and that she was used to this, and that it did not seem strange to her. People she had never met came up and began to speak to her in shopping malls, in elevators, in the waiting rooms of doctors, at traffic lights, at concerts, at coffee shops and bistros. An old man took hold of her arm outside of an amusement park and began whispering about his murdered son. A woman carrying three children placed her blanket right on top of theirs at the beach, stretched out next to Mrs. Mitchell, and began to cry. Even their dog, a stray she fed while camping in Tennessee, came scratching outside their door six weeks later. Mr. Mitchell was jealous and frightened by these strangers, and often used himself as a shield between them and his wife. *What do they want from her?* he found himself thinking. But he also felt, *What will they take from me?*

His wife was a quiet woman, in the way that large rocks just beyond the shore are quiet; the waves rush against them and the seaweed hangs on and the birds gather round on top. Mr. Mitchell was amazed that she had married him. He spent the first few years doing what he could to please her and watched for signs that she was leaving.

Sometimes she got depressed and locked herself in the bathroom. It made him furious. When she came out, tender and pink from washing, she would put her arms around him and tell him that he was a good man. Mr. Mitchell was not sure of this, because sometimes he found himself hating her. He wanted her to know what it felt like to be powerless. He began taking risks.

When he got the call from Venezuela telling him about Miguel, he was terrified that he might lose his wife and also secretly happy to have wounded her. But all of the control he felt as they prepared for his son's arrival slipped away as he watched her take the strange dark boy into her arms and tenderly wash his feet. He realized then that she was capable of taking everything from him.

The three of them formed an awkward family. Mr. Mitchell tried to place the boy in a home, but his wife would not let him. He had now been an accidental father for two years. He took the boy to baseball games and bought him comic books and drove him to school in the mornings. Sometimes Mr. Mitchell enjoyed these things; other times they made him angry. One day he walked in on Miguel talking to his wife in Spanish and the boy immediately stopped. He saw that his son was afraid of him, and he was sure that his wife had done this too. Mr. Mitchell began to resent what had initially drawn him to her, and to offset these feelings he began an affair with their neighbor, Pat.

It did not begin innocently. Pat said hello to Mr. Mitchell at the supermarket, then turned and pressed up against him as someone passed in the aisle. Her behind lingered against his hips, her breasts touched his arm. Mr. Mitchell had never had any conversation with Pat that went beyond the weather or the scheduling of trash, but later that week he walked over to her as she was planting bulbs in her garden and slid his hand into the elastic waistband of her Bermuda shorts. He leaned her up against the fence, underneath a birch tree, right there in the middle of a bright, sunny day where everyone could see. Mr. Mitchell didn't say anything, but he could tell by her breath and the way she rocked on his hand that she wasn't afraid.

He did not know it was in him to do something like this. He had been on his way to the library to return some books. Look, there they were, thrown aside on the grass, wrapped in plastic smeared with age and the fingers of readers who were unknown to him. And here was another person he did not know, panting in his ear, streaking his arms with dirt. Someone he had seen bent over in the sunlight, a slight glistening of sweat reflecting in the backs of her knees, and for whom he had suddenly felt a hard sense of lonesomeness and longing. A new kind of warmth spread in the palm of his hand and he tried not to think about his wife.

They had hard, raw sex in public places—movie theaters and parks, elevators and playgrounds. After dark, underneath the jungle gym, his knees pressing into the dirt, Mr. Mitchell began to wonder why they hadn't been caught. Once, sitting on a bench near the reservoir, Pat straddling him in a skirt with no underwear, they had actually waved to an elderly couple passing by. The couple continued on as if they hadn't seen them. The experience left the impression that his meetings with Pat were occurring in some kind of alternative reality, a bubble in time that he knew would eventually pop.

Pat told him that Clyde had been impotent since his father died. The old man had been a mechanic, and was working underneath a bulldozer when the lift slipped, crushing him from the chest down. Clyde held his father's hand as he died, and the coldness that came as life left seemed to spread through Clyde's fingers and into his arms, and he stopped using them to reach for his wife. Since the funeral she'd had two lovers. Mr. Mitchell was number three.

There were rumors, later on, that the lift had been tampered with—that Clyde's father had owed someone money. Pat denied it, but Mr. Mitchell remembered driving by the garage and sensing he'd rather buy his gas somewhere else. It seemed like a shady business.

He started arranging meetings with Pat that were closer to home. Mr. Mitchell's desire increased with the risk of discovery, and in his house he began to fantasize about the dining room table, the dryer in the laundry room, the space on the kitchen counter beside the mixer. He touched these places with his fingertips and trembled, thinking of how he would feel later, watching his wife sip her soup, fold shets, mix batter for cookies in the same places.

On the day Pat was murdered, before she put the roast in the oven or reminisced about James Dean or thought about the difference between butter and margarine, she was having sex in the vestibule. The coiled inscription of HOME SWEET HOME scratched her behind. Mr. Mitchell had seen Clyde leave for a bowling lesson, and as he waited on the front porch for Pat to open the door, some-thing had made him pick up the welcome mat. Mrs. Mitchell would soon be home with Miguel, and the thought of her so close pricked his ears. When Pat answered he'd thrown the mat down in the hall, then her, then himself, the soles of his shoes knocking over the entry table. Mr. Mitchell brought Pat's knees to his shoulders and listened for the hum of his wife's Reliant.

The following day when Lieutenant Sales climbed the stairs of Pat and Clyde's porch, he did not notice that there was nothing to wipe his feet on. He was an average-looking man: six foot two, 190 pounds, brown hair, brown eyes, brown skin. He had once been a champion deep-sea diver, until a shark attack (which left him with a hole in his side crossed with the pink, puckered scars of new skin) dragged him from the waters with a sense of righteous authority and induced him to join the force. He lived thirty-five minutes away in a basement apartment with a Siamese cat named Frank.

When Sales was a boy he'd had a teacher who smelled like roses. Her name was Mrs. Bosco. She showed him how to blow eggs. Forcing the yolk out of the tiny hole always felt a little disgusting, like blowing a heavy wad of snot from his nose, but when he looked up at Mrs. Bosco's cheeks flushed red with effort, he knew it would be worth it, and it was—the empty shell in his hand like a held breath. Whenever he began an investigation, he'd get the same sensation, and as he stepped into the doorway of Pat and Clyde's house, he felt it rise in his chest and stay.

He interviewed the police who found the bodies first. They were sheepish about their reasons for going into the backyard, but before long they

34

began loudly discussing drywall and Sheetrock and the pros and cons of lancet windows (all of the men, including Lieutenant Sales, carried weekend and part-time jobs in construction). The policeman who had thrown up in the bushes went home early. When Sales spoke to him later, he apologized for contaminating the scene.

Lieutenant Sales found the roast on the counter. He found green beans still on the stove. He found a sour cherry pie nearly burned in the oven. He found the butter and the margarine half-melted on the dining room table. He found that Pat and Clyde used cloth napkins and tiny separate plates for their dinner rolls. The silverware was polished. The edges of the steak knives were turned in.

He found their unpaid bills in a basket by the telephone. He found clean laundry inside the dryer in the basement—towels, sheets, T-shirts, socks, three sets of Fruit of the Loom and one pair of soft pink satin panties, the elastic starting to give, the bottom frayed and thin. He found an unfinished letter Pat had started writing to a friend who had recently moved to Arizona: *What is it like there? How can you stand the heat?* He found Clyde's stamp albums from when he was a boy—tiny spots of brilliant color, etchings of flowers and portraits of kings, painstakingly pasted over the names of countries Lieutenant Sales had never heard of.

He found the bullet that had passed through Pat's body, embedded in the stairs. He found a run in her stocking, starting at the heel and inching its way up the back of her leg. He thought about how Pat had been walking around the day she was going to die not realizing that there was a hole in her panty hose. He found a stain, dark and blooming beneath her shoulders, spreading across the Oriental rug in the foyer and into the hardwood floors, which he noticed, as he got down on his knees for a closer look, still held the scent of Murphy's oil soap. He found a hairpin caught in the carpet fringe. He found a cluster of dandelion seeds, the tiny white filaments coming apart in his fingers. He found a look on Pat's face like a child trying to be brave, lips tightened and thin, forehead just beginning to crease, eyes glazed, dark, and unconvinced. Her body was stiff when they moved her.

There were dog tracks on the back porch. They were the prints of a midsized animal, red and clearly defined as they circled the body in the kitchen, then crisscrossing over themselves and heading out the door, fading down the steps and onto the driveway before disappearing into the yard. Lieutenant Sales sent a man to knock on doors in the neighborhood and find out who let their dogs off the leash. He interviewed Clyde's mother. He went back to the station and checked Pat's and Clyde's records—both clean. When he finally went to sleep that night, the small warmth of his cat tucked next to his shoulder, Lieutenant Sales thought about the feel of satin panties, missing slippers, stolen welcome mats, dandelion seeds from a yard with no dandelions, and the kind of killer who shuts off the oven.

A month before Pat and Clyde were murdered, Mrs. Mitchell was fixing the toilet. Her husband passed by on his way to the kitchen, paused at the door, shook his head, and told her that she was too good for him. The heavy porcelain top was off, her arms elbow deep in rusty water. The man she had married was standing at the entrance to the bathroom and speaking, but Mrs. Mitchell was concentrating on the particular tone in the pipes she was trying to clear, and so she did not respond.

Mr. Mitchell went into the kitchen and began popping pop-corn. The kernels cracked against the insides of the kettle as his words settled into her, and when, with a twist of the coat hanger in her hand beneath the water, she stopped the ringing of the pipes, Mrs. Mitchell sensed in the quiet that came next that her husband had done something wrong. She had known in this same way before he told her about Miguel. A breeze came through the window and made the hair on her wet arms rise. She pulled her hands from the toilet and thought, *I fixed it.*

When Miguel came into their home, she had taken all the sorrow she felt at his existence and turned it into a fierce motherly love. Mrs. Mitchell thought her husband would be grateful; instead he seemed to hold it against her. He became dodgy and spiteful. He blamed her for what he'd done, for being a woman too hard to live up to. It was the closest she ever came to leaving. But she hadn't expected the boy.

Miguel spent the first three months of his life in America asking to go home. When the fourth month came he began to sleepwalk. He wandered downstairs to the kitchen, emptied the garbage can onto the floor, and curled up inside. In the morning Mrs. Mitchell would find him asleep, shoulders in the barrel, feet in the coffee grounds and leftovers. He told her he was looking for his mother's head. She had been decapitated in the bus accident, and now she stepped from the corners of Miguel's dreams at night and beckoned him with her arms, his lost chickens resting on her shoulders, pecking at the empty neck.

Mrs. Mitchell suggested that they make her a new one. She bought materials for papier-mâché. The strips of newspaper felt like bandages as she helped Miguel dip them in glue and smooth them over the surface of the inflated balloon. They fashioned a nose and lips out of cardboard. Once it was dry, Miguel described his mother's face and they painted the skin brown, added yarn for hair, cut eyelashes out of construction paper. Mrs. Mitchell took a pair of gold earrings, poked them through where they'd drawn the ears and said, heart sinking, *She's beautiful.* Miguel nodded. He smiled. He put his mother's head on top of the bookcase in his room and stopped sleeping in the garbage.

Sometimes when Mrs. Mitchell checked on the boy at night, she'd feel the head looking at her. It was unnerving. She imagined her husband making love to the papier-mâché face and discovered a hate so strong and hard it made her afraid of herself. She considered swiping the head and destroying it, but she remembered how skinny and pitiful the boy's legs had looked against her kitchen floor. Then Miguel began to love her, and she suddenly felt capable of anything. She thumbed her nose at the face in the corner. She held her heart open.

Mrs. Mitchell had been raised by her aunts in a house near the river where her mother had drowned. The aunts were hunters; birds mostly, which they would clean and cook and eat. As a girl Mrs. Mitchell would retrieve the shots. Even on a clear day, the birds always seemed wet. Sometimes they were still alive when she found them—wings thrashing, pieces of their chests torn away. She learned to take hold of their necks and break them quickly.

Mrs. Mitchell kept a picture of her mother next to the mirror in her room, and whenever she checked her reflection, her eyes would naturally turn from her own face to that of the woman who gave birth to her. The photo was black-and-white and creased near the edges; she was fifteen, her hair plaited, the end of one braid pressed between her lips. It made Mrs. Mitchell think of stories she'd heard of women who spent their lives spinning—

years of passing flax through their mouths to make thread would leave them disfigured, lower lips drooping off their faces; a permanent look of being beaten.

The aunts built a shooting range on an area of property behind the house. It was Mrs. Mitchell's job to set up the targets and fetch them iced tea and ammo. She kept a glass jar full of shells in the back of her closet, shiny gold casings from her aunts' collection of .22 calibers and .45s. They made a shooting station out of an old shed, two tables set up with sandbags to hold the guns, nestling the shape of heavy metal as the pieces were placed down.

When she was twelve years old the aunts gave her a rifle. She already knew the shooting stances, and she practiced them with her new gun every day after school. She could hit a target while kneeling, crouching, lying down, and standing tall, hips parallel to the barrel and her waist turned, the same way the aunts taught her to pose when a picture was being taken. She picked off tin cans and old metal signs and polka-dotted the paper outlines of men.

Mrs. Mitchell remembered this when she pulled into her driveway, glanced over the fence, and saw her husband having sex in the doorway of their neighbors' house. She turned to Miguel in the passenger seat and told him to close his eyes. The boy covered his face with his hands and sat quietly while she got out of the car. Mrs. Mitchell watched her husband moving back and forth and felt her feet give way from the ground. She had the sensation of being caught in a river, the current pulling her body outward, tugging at her ankles, and she wondered why she wasn't being swept away until she realized that she was holding on to the fence. The wood felt smooth and worn, like the handle of her first gun, and she used it to pull herself back down.

Later she thought of the look on Pat's face. It reminded Mrs. Mitchell of the Tin Woodman from the movie *The Wizard of Oz*—disarmingly lovely and greasy with expectation. In the book version she bought for Miguel she'd read that the Woodman had once been real, but his ax kept slipping and he'd dismembered himself, slowly exchanging his flesh piece by piece for hollow metal. Mrs. Mitchell thought Pat's body would rattle with the same kind of emptiness, but it didn't; it fell with the heavy tone of meat. As she waited for the echo, Mrs. Mitchell heard a small cough from the kitchen, the kind a person does in polite society to remind someone else that they are there. She followed it and found Clyde in his slippers, the knife in the roast.

Hello. I just killed your wife. And when she said it, she knew she'd have to shoot Clyde too. The beans were boiling, the water frothing over the sides of the pan and sizzling into the low flame beneath. Mrs. Mitchell turned off the oven and spun all the burners to zero.

41

The aunts never married. They still lived in the house where they raised their niece. Occasionally they sent her photographs, recipes, information on the NRA, or obituaries of people she had known clipped from the local newspaper. When a reporter called Mrs. Mitchell, asking questions about Pat and Clyde, she thought back to all the notices her aunts had sent over the years, and said: *They were good neighbors and wonderful people. I don't know who would have done something like this. They will be greatly missed.* The truth was that she felt very little for Pat. It was hard to forgive herself for this, so she didn't try. Instead she did her best to forget how Clyde had looked, the surprise on his face, as if he were about to offer her a drink before he crumpled to the floor.

She waited patiently through the following day for someone to come for her. She watched the police cruisers and the news vans come and go. On Monday morning she woke up and let the dog out. She made a sandwich for Miguel and fit it in his lunch box beside a thermos of milk. She poured juice into a glass and cereal into a bowl. Then she locked herself in the bathroom and watched her hands shake. She remembered that she had wanted to cover Clyde with something. Falling out of the box, the cereal had sounded crisp and new like water on rocks, but it quickly turned into a soggy mess that stayed with her as she left him, stepped over Pat, and picked up the welcome mat with her gloves. She could still see

42

her husband moving back and forth on top of it. She wanted to make HOME SWEET HOME disappear, but the longest she could bring herself to touch it was the end of the driveway, and she left it in a garbage can on the street.

She found that she could not say good-bye. Not when her husband pounded on the door to take a shower and not when Miguel asked if he could brush his teeth. She sat on the toilet and listened to them move about the house and leave. Later, she watched through the window as a man wrapped her neighbors' house in police tape. To double it around a tree in the yard, he circled the trunk with his arms. It was a brief embrace and she thought, *That tree felt nothing.*

In the afternoon, when the sun began to slant, Lieutenant Sales crossed the Mitchells' front yard. He was carrying a chewed-up slipper in a bag, jostling the dandelions, and sending seeds of white fluff adrift. Mrs. Mitchell saw him coming. She turned the key in the lock, and once she was beyond the bathroom, she ran her fingers through her hair, smoothing down the rough spots. The bell rang. The dog barked. She opened the door, and offered him coffee.

Miguel turned nine that summer. In the past two years he'd spent with the Mitchells, the boy had grown no more than an inch; but with the warm weather that June, he'd suddenly sprouted—his legs stretching like brown sugar taffy tight over his new knobby bones, as if the genes of his American father had been lying dormant, biding their time until the right combination of spring breezes and processed food kissed them awake. He began to trip over himself. On his way home from baseball practice that Monday, he caught one of his newly distended feet on a trash can just outside the line of police tape that closed in Pat and Clyde's yard. Miguel fell to the sidewalk, smacking his hands against the concrete. The barrel toppled over beside him, and out came a welcome mat. HOME SWEET HOME.

Miguel was not the best student, but he had made friends easily once he hit several home runs in gym class. Norman and Greg Kessler, twins and the most popular kids in school, chose him for their team and for their friend. Norman and Greg helped him with his English, defended him against would-be attackers, and told him when they saw his father naked.

Mr. Mitchell had driven past them on the highway, stripped bare from the waist down. From the window of their mother's minivan, Norman and Greg could see a woman leaning over the gearshift. *It's true*, said the twins. Miguel made them swear on the Bible, on a stack of Red Sox cards, and finally on their grandfather's grave, which they did, bikes thrown aside in the grass and sweaty hands pressed on the polished marble of his years. At dinner that night the boy watched his father eating. The angle of his jaw clenched and turned.

Miguel felt a memory push past hot dogs, past English, past Hostess cupcakes and his collection of Spiderman comic books. He was five years old and asked his mother where his father was. She was making coffee—squeezing the grounds through a sieve made out of cloth and wire. He'd collected eggs from their chickens for breakfast. He was holding them in his hands and they were still warm. His mother took one from him. *This is the world and we are here*, she said, and pointed to the bottom half of the egg. *Your father is there.* She ran her finger up along the edge and tapped the point with a dark red nail. Then she cracked the yolk in a pan and threw the rest of the egg in the garbage. He retrieved it later and pushed his fingertips back and forth across the slippery inner membrane until the shell came apart into pieces.

Miguel picked up the doormat and shook it to get the dust off. It seemed like something Mrs. Mitchell might be fond of. That morning he had kept watch through the bathroom keyhole. She was out of sight, but he could sense her worry.

In Caracas he had gone through the trash regularly, looking for things to play with and at times for something to eat. Ever since he heard about his father being naked on the highway, he had been remembering more about his life there, and even reverting to some of his old habits, as if the non sequitur of his father's nudity had tenderly shaken him awake. He lay in bed at night and looked into the eyes of the papier-mâché head for guidance. He had two lives now, two countries and two mothers. Soon he would find another life without his father, and another, when he went away to college, and another life, and another, and another, and another, each of them a thin, fragile casing echoing the hum of what had gone before.

The boy walked into the kitchen and found his American mother sitting with a strange man. They both held steaming mugs of coffee. Buster was under the table, waking from his afternoon nap. He saw Miguel and thumped his tail halfheartedly against the floor. The adults turned. *Now, what have you got there?*

Lieutenant Sales took HOME SWEET HOME in his hands. There was something in the look of the boy and the feel of the rope that held possibility, and the twisted pink skin where the shark had bitten him began to itch. It had been tingling all afternoon. Later, in the lab, the welcome mat would reveal tiny spots of Pat's blood, dog saliva, gunpowder, dead ants, mud, fertilizer, and foot-prints—but not the impression of Mr. Mitchell's knees, or the hesitation of his jealous wife on the doorstep, or the hunger of his son in the garbage. All of this had been shaken off.

Lieutenant Sales would leave the Mitchell's house that afternoon with the same thrill he'd had when the shark passed and he realized his leg was still there. He was exhilarated and then exhausted, as though his life had been drained, and he knew then that he had gone as far as he could go. There would be no scar and no solution to the murder, just the sense that he had missed something, and the familiar taste of things not done. For now, he reached out with a kind of hope and accepted the welcome mat as a gift.

Mrs. Mitchell put her arm around Miguel's shoulders and waited for Lieutenant Sales to arrest her. She would continue to wait in the weeks ahead as suspects were raised and then dismissed and headlines changed and funerals were planned. The possibilities of these moments passed over her like shadows. When they were gone she was left standing chilled.

Clyde's mother arranged for closed caskets. In the pew Mrs. Mitchell sat quietly. Her husband looked nervous and cracked knuckles. After the service they went home and Mr. Mitchell started to pack. His wife listened to the suitcases being dragged down from the attic, the swing of hangers, zipper teeth, the straps of leather buckles. Mr. Mitchell said he was leaving, and his wife felt her throat clutch. She wanted to ask him where he would go; she wanted to ask him what she had done this for; she wanted to ask him why he no longer loved her, but instead she asked for his son.

She had watched Miguel hand the frayed rope to the detective, and as it passed by her, she felt an ache in the back of her mouth as though she hadn't eaten for days. Lieutenant Sales turned HOME SWEET HOME over in his hands. He placed it carefully on the kitchen table and Mrs. Mitchell saw the word *Sweet*. She remembered the milk she had made for the boy when he arrived, and sensed that this would not be the end of her. She could hear the steady breathing of her sleeping dog. She could smell the coffee. She felt the small frame of Miguel steady beneath her hand. These bones, she thought, were everything. *Hey, sport,* Mrs. Mitchell asked, *is that for me?* The boy nodded, and she held him close.

REASONABLE TERMS

It began with a list of demands, presented to the zookeeper. This had taken some time to prepare. The giraffes had to explain their situation to one of the mountain gorillas in the neighboring pen, and after intense negotiations (a percentage of food to be delivered in three installments: one-third upon translation, one-third upon contact with the gorilla's sign language tutor, and the final one-third upon receipt of the document), the giraffes had procured their list. In an appropriately dramatic gesture, their elected spokesanimal, Doë, approached the wire enclosure of their pen while the keeper was conducting a tour of the zoo for potential benefactors, and gracefully stretching her neck over the edge of the fence, she delicately laid the paper across the zookeeper's balding head with her teeth.

At first the zookeeper tried to laugh off the incident as a prank played on him by one of his favorite animals. But as he began to glance over said document, his ears turned red and a blush crept up across his neck like a rash. In bold, stiff lettering that the sign language tutor, a vexed woman in her mid-thirties, felt was appropriate to the occasion, the letter made the following statement:

DEAR ZOOKEEPER:

BEING ONE OF THE BIGGEST ATTRACTIONS AT THE ZOO (PROVIDING EIGHT PERCENT OF NET GROSS INCOME YEARLY), AS WELL AS MAKING THE TOP TEN LIST OF FAVORITE ANIMALS THREE YEARS IN A ROW, WE, THE UNDERSIGNED, HAVE RESORTED TO THE ATTACHED LIST OF DEMANDS IN RESPONSE TO THE INACTION ON YOUR PART IN PREVIOUS NEGOTIATIONS, NAMELY: ENLARGEMENT OF PEN, ALTERATIONS IN DIET, AND VIOLATION OF PRIVACY ACT 76865 CODE E. IF OUR DEMANDS CONTINUE TO BE IGNORED BY YOUR OFFICE, WE WILL BE FORCED TO TAKE NECESSARY ACTION TO ENSURE OUR RIGHTS, WHICH WERE STATED IN OUR PRELIMINARY CONTRACT.

SINCERELY,
DOË
LULU
FRANCESCO

DEMANDS

1. **TOO MUCH ACACIA.** ALTHOUGH WE ARE IMPORTED AMERICANS, WE TOO WOULD

LIKE TO SAVOR THE MIX OF CULTURES. HOW ABOUT SOME WISTERIA? BAMBOO? COMBRETUM? OR MAPLE LEAVES? LET'S HAVE A LITTLE CACTUS.

2. **A BIGGER PEN**. THE VERTICAL MUST BE IN CORRESPONDENCE TO THE HORIZONTAL. THE OKAPI ARE ALLOTTED ONE HUNDRED SQUARE FEET MORE THAN WE ARE, AS NOTED IN PREVIOUS COMPLAINTS. UNDUE PRIVILEGES HAVE CONSISTENTLY BEEN GIVEN TO THE OKAPI FOR THEIR PARTICI-PATION IN THE 'MINI' FAD, ALL OF WHICH HAVE BEEN REPORTED AND ITEMIZED IN ADDENDUM A OF THIS DOCUMENT.

3. **PRIVACY**. DUE TO OBVIOUS PHYSICAL ATTRIBUTES, PRIVATE MOMENTS ARE SUBJECT TO CONSTANT SUPERVISION. A SECTION OF HIGH TREES (TWENTY-FIVE FEET OR MORE) PLANTED IN THE REAR QUADRANT OF OUR PEN WOULD PROVIDE RELIEF, SOLITUDE, A NOOK OF OUR OWN.

4. **QUALITY OF LIFE**. WE LIVE IN A WORLD DETERMINED BY YOUR BORDERS. BUT OUR GIFTS OF NATURE SUPPLY US WITH THE ABILITY TO SEE BEYOND THESE LINES TO BETTER THINGS. AUTOMATED SPRIN-KLER SYSTEMS. TWENTY-FOUR-HOUR CONVENIENCE STORES. THE SUCCULENT, ABUNDANT FOLIAGE OF THE NEWLAND ARBORETUM (LOCATED FIVE MILES SOUTHWEST OF OUR ENCLOSURE). ALL

THESE THINGS MAKE US DESIRE A MORE
TEXTURED EXPERIENCE. A GREATER TO-
MORROW. AN EXPANSION OF OUR EXIS-
TENCE. THE POSSIBILITY OF ICE CREAM.

P.S. BEWARE. DUE TO OUR FRAGILE CARDIO-
VASCULAR SYSTEMS, IT IS DANGEROUS TO
EXCITE US.

The zookeeper was not tickled by this disclo-
sure. In fact, he was rather displeased. The giraffes
were old reliables. They'd been part of the zoo
since he started as a dung sweeper in high school.
He had other things to worry about—a sick musk
ox, the exhibit of South American tree frogs, and
Disney. He folded the list of demands, slipped it
into his front pocket, and steered the group of
benefactors toward the emus.

This was not the reaction anticipated by the
giraffes. It had been two years since the morning
when, over a breakfast of acacia leaves, Doë had
turned to Francesco and said she believed their lives
were not what they could be. The giraffes had spent
the next year and a half debating the pros and cons
of declaring their dissatisfaction. The procurement
of the document had taken four months. The
gorilla's payment was costly—his response time,
grueling. The opportunity to present it to the
director of the zoo had been a wait of thirteen weeks.
They had been patient, and his apparent disregard
for their wants and feelings and his dismissal of their

threat (which Lulu had insisted they include in order to be taken seriously and, as she put it, "capture their mood") was keenly felt.

After a catered luncheon with the patrons by the lion pit, the zookeeper returned to his office. He took the giraffes' list of demands out of his pocket and spread it on his desk, smoothing it with his fingers. He knew that word of this would soon spread to the other animals, and he recognized the possibility of a disruption.

The zookeeper often compared management of the zoo to marriage with his wife, Matilda. She was a large, angry woman he'd met while traveling through Romania. He was often afraid of her. But he was also fascinated by her brooding and the thickness of where her legs met the beginnings of her behind. Early in their marriage, he discovered that the tone of authority was calming for Matilda. After barking a sharp retort, he could see her shoulders loosen and give way. He would follow this with kindness (sweet things he would like to smother her in), and he found it was only in these moments that she would accept his love. He tried to imagine what he would do if Matilda gave him a list of demands. He would tear it up in her face. He would try to convince her that he was angry. He would scream obscenities, shake his fist, then secretly make sure everything she desired came true.

The zookeeper decided the best action would be to publicly refuse the giraffes' demands.

Perhaps even to make an initial show of punishment so the other animals would realize what defiance would cost them. He couldn't have every species writing lists and such. What, for example, would the hippos demand? Or the wombats? After the situation blew over, in a few months, perhaps a year, he could then begin to implement some of the less costly modifications, make the animals believe the gesture came from his own good nature, and make the benefactors believe he was an impetus of change. The zookeeper smiled to himself and opened the drawer of his file cabinet to the appropriate letter. As he fingered the G, his secretary buzzed through the intercom. She told him that a hysterical groundsman was on the line and that all of the giraffes were dead.

The giraffes had concluded that the surest way to get a response to their demands was to sabotage the zoo's usage of them. A mock group suicide, they decided, would bring the greatest attention to their cause. Francesco, Lulu, and Doë stretched themselves on the ground, stuck their legs in the air, stared blankly, twisted their necks at severe angles, and hung their long black tongues out of the sides of their mouths.

It was not long before the children began to cry. Horrified parents, teachers, and babysitters ran for the exits, afraid of scarring their innocent charges with further sightings of animal corpses, and muttered, *This never would have happened at Disney.*

The zookeeper was rushed to the scene by golf cart.

"What's all this?" he said. "What's going on here?" A crowd of zoologists, groundsmen, and adults who were visiting the zoo without children that day were pressed against the safety railing that surrounded the fence, which surrounded the pen, which surrounded the bodies of the giraffes.

"They're alive," said one of the zoologists. "I can see them breathing."

"Let's turn the hoses on them," said the groundsman who had called the zookeeper. He was no longer hysterical.

"They might be sick," said the zoologist, "or depressed. We should bring in a psychiatrist."

"I'm a psychiatrist," said one of the adults without children. "And it's plain to see these giraffes have been abused. I'm going to contact the SPCA and have them removed from this environment immediately."

The zookeeper closed his eyes. He thought of Matilda. He tried to imagine what he would do if he came home and found her pretending to be dead. He pictured her enormous body supine on the floor of their kitchen, her legs twisted beneath her and one eye open, gauging his reaction. How furious he would be! How dare she pretend to take herself from him! For the first time in his life he felt pure rage with no lingering fear or trepidation. He was about to tell the groundsmen to blast the giraffes to pieces with the hoses, when one of the zoologists moved slightly, and he saw into the pen.

Lulu and Doë were on their sides, their necks bent forward so that their heads rested on their hooves. Both had their tongues hanging in the dirt, and every few moments Lulu's tail seemed to twitch. Francesco was balanced on his back—his neck straight—his two front legs curled into his chest, and his two back legs sticking eight feet into the air in a V formation. Francesco had his head turned toward the spectators behind the fence and his lower jaw twisted in what he supposed was an accurate representation of the anguish of death.

The giraffes' bodies extended across their pen. They seemed to take up every inch of earth. They were enormous, prehistoric. The zookeeper looked at the animals prostrate in the dirt and was reminded of pre-Darwinian concepts of evolution—that the length of giraffes' necks was determined by stretching to obtain what they desired. He wondered if this kind of despair was inside Matilda. In his mind he picked her up from the floor of their kitchen and laid her beside the giraffes. As he imagined Matilda on the ground before him, her feigned death became horribly real. He felt a sharp pain in his left arm, spreading through his shoulder and across his chest. His eyes filled with tears. He flung himself from the golf cart and onto a patch of grass.

Reporters arrived on the scene. They had received dozens of calls regarding the collapse of family entertainment. They snapped photos of the zoo-keeper sobbing on the grass. They snapped the zoologist and the groundsman wrestling over the hose. They snapped a portrait of the psychiatrist looking grim. Then they snapped the giraffes.

The reporters rushed out of the zoo to make the evening paper with their headlines:

GIRAFFES FAKE OWN DEATH. ZOOKEEPER DISTRAUGHT OVER CRIMES AGAINST NATURE. PSYCHIATRIST TALKS ANIMALS OUT OF MASS SUICIDE. HOSE IS TO BLAME?

From his hospital room at Saint Sebastian's, the zookeeper puts in a call to the benefactors. He has sustained a mild heart attack. Tiny metal elec-trodes from a monitor stick to the hair on his chest. His wife, Matilda, is by his side. He is nervous when she is not with him. She knows this, and when he sleeps, she tucks a corner of her skirt into his hand.

Matilda holds the phone receiver to the zookeeper's mouth as he reads off the list of demands. On the other end of the line, there is silence. The benefactors are not happy. The nega-tive publicity has already affected ticket sales at the zoo. Citizens, outraged at the photographs of "dead" giraffes, are organizing a boycott. There is talk of scruples, and rumors of investigations. The benefactors are angry at having been put in this position by the giraffes. They tell the zookeeper not to release the demands to the public. This is not the time to renegotiate contracts, they say. What we need is damage control.

Side by side in their pen, in their third day of protest, Doë, Lulu, and Francesco discuss their odds. Francesco is losing hope. The zoo has installed portable fences in front of the giraffes' pen to keep the protesters hidden. Francesco is upset that the public can no longer see his performance. He misses his view. He is tired of ants crawling up his nose and longs to climb to his feet.

Doë is not bothered by being so close to the ground. She feels more a part of the nature of things than ever before. She is confident their demands will be heard and met. She believes they all must be patient.

Lulu says nothing. She can feel her heart working. She imagines the blood flowing through her body horizontally. *What fun*, she thinks, *it must be having. Such an easy time moving where it wants to go.* When the day is over and the zoo closes, she hesitates in the last moment before rising to her feet.

The benefactors hold a press conference. We are happy people, they say. We want our animals happy too. They announce their decision to hire the psychiatrist, who subsequently drops the suit he was bringing against them on behalf of the giraffes by the SPCA. The psychiatrist spends several days in the giraffes' pen, sitting in a chair, pulling at his mustache, and taking notes on a yellow legal pad. He informs the benefactors that the giraffes are understimulated, and gives an impassioned plea for entertainment. The benefactors contact the Guild of Nightclub Performers and comprise a rotating list of magicians, impersonators, and cabaret acts.

The portable fences in front of the giraffes' pen are removed and replaced with star trailers, stage lights, and PA equipment. Benches are installed for zoo visitors to enjoy the show. The first showcase combines Judy Garland impersonators, the juggling Marconis, and a Gilbert and Sullivan revue. Coffee, doughnuts, and free passes are provided for all the newspaper reporters. The headlines begin to change.

Francesco is pleased. Their case, he feels, is finally getting the attention it deserves. He finds the nightclub performers delightful and develops an affinity for sequins.

Doë is annoyed. All of the commotion is disrupting her communion with nature. She wonders at this mix of protest and cabaret. *Why haven't they given us trees?* she thinks. *Where is our wisteria?*

Lulu remains calm. This daily horizontal ritual has begun to change her. Sometimes she will phase out into a dreamlike state, have visions, and talk to God. It begins with a flash of blue light; her body starts to tremble. She has a sense of lift; she feels her body rise and float, and suddenly she finds herself out of the zoo, moving across the city, between buildings, over traffic, gliding by apartment windows. She looks in at people cooking dinner, watching television, talking on the telephone. She sees a man singing opera in the shower. The echoing, bellowing sound seems to carry across the air directly into her ears. When she comes to, Lulu is back on the ground, in the dirt, and she is full of wonder at what she has seen. She makes several attempts to inform the others, but they refuse to believe her. Doë worries that Lulu may be losing her mind, and Francesco wonders if the groundsmen have started to drug their food.

By the second week of protest, the doughnuts have gone stale and the reporters are looking for an ending. The public interest in suicidal giraffes is waning. The giraffes' story has moved from the front page to the Metro section to a short column in Living. The Guild of Nightclub Performers has played out its contract and packed its bags. The reporters dust the powdered sugar from their fingers and begin to look for new assignments.

Through quick wit and skill, the benefactors have averted a PR disaster. Now they decide the time has come for a fast and sure resolution of the crisis. Discreetly they inquire about how to get some fresh giraffes. Calls are made; prices are bargained. The benefactors obtain three new giraffes from a California zoo in exchange for two warthogs, a flying squirrel, and a sum of money raised from the sale of Doë, Lulu, and Francesco to a traveling circus that asks no questions.

The benefactors send a telegram to the zookeeper at the hospital, informing him that a miracle will occur. In the morning when the zoo opens, there will be three healthy, reasonable, slightly disoriented giraffes making their way delicately across their new surroundings on twelve perfect little hooves.

Lulu has another vision. Floating across the city, she passes Saint Sebastian's. She glides by the zookeeper's window and notices him in a hospital bed, propped up, asleep, and covered with electrodes. She can see Matilda by the bed, knitting, her skirt hitched to the side, a corner tucked into the zookeeper's hand. Matilda has a kerchief tied around her head; her eyes are set fixedly on the needles working back and forth. The window is open a crack and Lulu hovers closer. She tips her nose against it, and clouds the pane with her breath.

Inside the zookeeper's hospital room, the needles click and the heart monitor beeps. The zookeeper is dreaming in time—the sound becomes a train moving along a track. Click click beep. Click click beep. Lulu follows this rhythm into the zookeeper's dream and discovers the boxcar of a traveling circus. Inside she finds Matilda, curled up on a pile of straw. There is no air, no water, in the boxcar. Matilda is pressing her mouth against a crack in the wood. She is trying to breathe; her lips are full of splinters. Lulu is afraid. She feels the zookeeper's hands go weak and watches as Matilda's skirt slips from his fingers.

The zookeeper wakes. He reaches up and pulls the electrodes off his chest, throws back the covers on his hospital bed, and says, "I have to do something." His legs look white and thin. He grabs hold of Matilda to steady himself as he climbs out of the bed.

Lulu takes a deep breath. She watches Matilda help the zookeeper button his pajamas. *There is something else here,* she thinks. A part of the dream is lingering. She tries to catch the scent of it, inhaling and exhaling, searching the hospital room. Suddenly she recognizes the smell—it is the chemical used in the tranquilizer darts that brought her down in Africa. It seems to close around her, and Lulu feels herself slipping away from the zookeeper and Matilda. She remembers the boom, the sting of the needles, and how the heaviness of her body pulled her to the ground.

Lulu opens her eyes. She is back in the zoo, on the floor of the pen. Through the darkness she senses movement. A crowd of figures is climbing through the safety railing. Lulu's long black tongue feels dry and unfamiliar—she cannot make it form a sound. She turns her head and sees Francesco and Doë begin to run. There is a shower of cracks, Lulu sees the glint of the darts, and the two giraffes fall like trees.

A large truck backs up to the pen. The tailgate is opened and a ramp slides out. Lulu watches as the groundsmen from the zoo begin to prepare her friends for loading. She tries to stand. She lifts her head and begins to feel dizzy. Her legs are shaking; she no longer remembers how to make them carry her away.

A golf cart appears. In it is the zookeeper, still in

his hospital pajamas. Matilda drives. Puffing behind in a lopsided run are several rotund newspaper reporters—the last to abandon the free coffee and doughnuts are the first to break the story on the illegal giraffe market. The bulbs on their cameras send streaks through the darkness. There is a flash of Doë's body covered with ropes. A flash of Francesco dazed and sedated. A flash of Lulu lying on her side. A flash of the groundsmen running away, their uniforms hazy reflections in the distance.

With the help of Matilda, the zookeeper steps out of the golf cart. He hesitates, not because he is afraid, but because he is embarrassed at being seen in his pajamas. Matilda realizes this and hands him the scarf she knitted in the hospital. He thanks her and pulls it across his shoulders.

The zookeeper walks over to where the giraffes are lying on the ground. He can hear them breathing. He crouches next to Lulu and tentatively touches the side of her neck. The hair is short and coarse; it feels like the welcome mat on his front porch at home. Lulu opens her eyes. She recognizes the zookeeper, and thinks she is having another vision. She remembers the metal wires connected to his chest, and the smell of the chemical darts surrounding him. How are you feeling, she tries to say, but instead her head turns, her mouth opens, and her long black tongue reaches out and strokes the zookeeper's hand.

PRESERVATION

There is a family on the other side of the glass. Mary lifts her paintbrush and starts to wave, but of course they are looking at the lion, not at her. The stuffed animal's teeth are bared, its claws digging into a plastic zebra leg, silicone foam drooling from the corner of its mouth. The daughter in the family, a small red-haired girl, flattens her nose next to the museum sign that says *Pardon Our Appearance.*

The father picks up the daughter and pantomimes throwing her into the lion's den, which elicits screams that Mary cannot hear, followed by an animated reprimand from the mother, who is pushing a stroller with another child in it—a boy, Mary guesses, from the trucks on the sleeve of his shirt. Chastened, the father puts the girl down, straightens the shirt that has ridden up over her belly. Just as the family is moving on to the next exhibit, he sees Mary standing near the trees and frowns.

She has been working on the mammal dioramas for the past week, having made her way through amphibians and reptiles. Mary did not go to art

69

school to work at a natural history museum, but this is where she has found herself. Her business started with a few murals in local restaurants. They were mostly nature scenes—mountains and rivers and underwater portraits that featured animals the customers would be having for dinner. A man named Harry Turner ate in one of these restaurants, enjoyed the mural, and hired her to paint three large-breasted sirens on the ceiling above his bathtub.

"I want the nipples rosy," he said. The tub was the size of a wading pool. Mary stood on the ladder and closed her eyes and found the color the way her father had taught her. She imagined the soft underside of petals, the silkiness between the layers. Harry Turner was so happy with the breasts that he made a few phone calls, recommended her to friends, business partners, and board members.

The work at the natural history museum is mostly in the late afternoons and evenings, when the school groups and tourists clear out of the marble hallways and begin to think about having dinner. Mary arrives at five o'clock, after her father's nurse takes over for the evening, and reports to Dr. Fisher, who is supervising the renovation.

Together they walk through the exhibition. They are supposed to be going over the progress she has made, but Dr. Fisher wants to talk about her father. "I wrote a paper on him in college," he says. "Did he really use brushes made out of his own hair?"

Mary smiles but does not answer. This is her usual response to comments about her father.

Sooner or later the speaker usually gets the hint and stops talking. Dr. Fisher does not. He is short and, as if to make up for this, quite muscular. The sleeves of his jacket fit snugly around his biceps. Mary towers over him, a beanpole.

He reminds her of a chemistry teacher she had in high school who was discovered, near the end of the year, to have been leading a double life as a professional bodybuilder. He had been such a quiet, simple-looking man that when a classmate handed her a photograph of him at a show, greased up, flexing in a thong, Mary shut her eyes, horribly embarrassed for him.

In the center of the hall is a large black bear posed on a pedestal outside the dioramas. The animal is on all fours, its head lifted as if something has just caught its attention, its behind round and large enough to fit a person inside. Dr. Fisher puts his hand on the bear's neck.

"I can't imagine what it's like to be related to him," he says. "This must seem so dull in comparison, repainting someone else's scenery."

"You didn't hire my father," says Mary.

The truth is working on the dioramas has been exciting. When she began sponging the years of dirt and grime from the landscape Michael Everett had painted seventy-five years earlier, Mary started to sweat. It wasn't the lighting, and it wasn't the lack of air inside the glass booth. It wasn't even the closeness of the stuffed animals, moved to the side so that she could have access to the wall. The heat seemed to be coming from the drawing itself, from the earth and trees of the Serengeti. Mary finished cleaning off a field of grasses and pressed her cheek against the wall. It was warm.

There is little information on Michael Everett in the orientation packet provided by Dr. Fisher. The photographs are blurry and the text obscure, but it is possible to discern that Everett was sick for most of his life. His body is thin and gaunt. There are shadows beneath his eyes, and in one picture there is a definite grimace, as if the flash from the camera pained him.

That night Mary reads through a history of the museum borrowed from the library. Everett was friends with the Roach family, who gave the original funding and land for the site, as well as their private collection of hunting trophies. There is a shot of him on safari with the whole clan. He is leaning on the shoulder of the youngest son. She holds the pictures up in front of her father.

"Do you know him, Pop?" she asks.

Her father shakes his head. He makes the smacking noise with his lips that means he is in trouble.

"Does it hurt?"

He nods. Mary takes out one of the prepared needles left by Mercedes, the hospice nurse, and pulls up his nightgown. With a grunt, her father turns, and she jabs the syringe into his small white flat buttock. Her father's paintings hang in the Whitney and the Museum of Modern Art.

Large canvases of abstract blues and greens, enveloping the viewer with emotion. There have been two books written about his life. He taught her how to mix colors, how to create perspective, and how to live without a mother. Now he wears a nightgown and lives from shot to shot.

A few minutes later her father is ready to talk. He sleeps for most of the day, but in the evenings, he needs distraction.

"What kind of artist was he?" her father asks.

"Landscape," Mary says.

"Let me see the picture again," he says. "Oh, yes. I've heard of him." Her father points at the youngest Roach son. "They were lovers."

"How do you know that?"

"Roach bought a few of my paintings. He made a pass at me once. Then he said Everett was the love of his life."

Mary looks at the photograph again. She imagines Roach in her father's studio over the Chinese noodle factory. All day and all night the sound of the machines drummed underneath the floor. Flour rose like steam through the airshaft. Her father created his best work in that space. She wasn't allowed to go inside unless he invited her.

Once, she went to the studio after locking herself out of their house and found him asleep in his cot with his arms around another man. The man was young, in his twenties, with a chest as smooth and hairless as a ten-year-old boy's. Lying so still side by side, their bodies looked as if they had been arranged for composition, the way an artist would display a bowl of fruit. Mary backed out slowly, her heart pounding, and the man opened his eyes. She was not supposed to be there, and the man in the bed seemed to know this, watching her lazily. Her father shifted in his sleep. The man did not move. Mary looked at him for a moment longer and then she closed the door.

Her father never brought his lovers to their house. He never introduced her to any of them. Since he became ill, he seemed to have forgotten that they had never discussed this.

"Look." Her father points at his leg. The skin is as thin as rice paper. Capillaries spread across in dark thin lines, intersecting like lace. The veins are thick and blue. "I've been thinking of donating my body to science."

"Please don't talk like that, Pop."

"Why not?"

"Because I don't want to think about you on a dissection table."

"I want to be useful," he says. "I'm sick of doing nothing."

Mary does not answer him. She has been caring for her father this way for a year. Living in the bedroom she left when she was eighteen. Visitors come when she is working. Dealers and friends of her father who, when she graduated from art school, politely declined to represent her work. At the time, her father had been furious. He wanted her to study in Italy for a year, but she knew, even then, that she would never be an artist; at least not an artist like him.

"How's Mercedes?" The nurse is their fallback conversation.

"She talks to her friends in Spanish on the phone. As if I don't understand." Mercedes is the only nurse in the area who can keep the hours. She is competent and resourceful and always on time, but neither of them likes her. Her father believes she is artless, and Mary is bothered by the way Mercedes touches him, as if he were a chair or a lamp.

"You don't speak Spanish."

"I might." He looks at her warily, enough to make her think that perhaps he does know how to speak Spanish. That this is just another one of the things he has kept hidden from her.

Among a herd of wildebeests in the migration diorama, she can see where the animals' joints are coming loose. The stitching shows. The noses are cracked, the horns precariously tilting. There are nine of them in the glass enclosure with her. Painted on the wall, in various sizes and degrees of perspective, there are perhaps five hundred more.

A group of teenage boys stops to peer in the window. They are thirteen at most—with thin arms and legs that are growing too fast to be strong. One of the boys points at her and they all turn, and Mary smiles, weakly. Their eyes travel over her body. A boy with sandy hair begins to tug at his belt. The other boys glance left and right, and then Sandy drops his pants and moons her.

The flash is brief, but in the moment when he connects his cheeks to the glass, she can see the unhealthy skin—the red bumps spreading across his lower back. Afterward the group scatters quickly. She can hear the echoes of their whoops down the hall.

She reports the boys to Dr. Fisher. He is standing on a stool, trying to reach a book on the upper shelf, when she walks into his office. He jumps down, and Mary can see that it makes him unhappy to be disturbed.

"How could they expose themselves without a teacher noticing?"

"I didn't see any teachers."

"Perhaps you imagined it."

Mary imagines her hands around Dr. Fisher's neck, but then she lets it go. She needs the job. Her father's medical expenses have drained their savings. As she walks through the hall, she slaps the black bear on the behind. She crawls into the migration diorama, picks up a brush, and paints a tiny caricature of Dr. Fisher in the corner, getting kicked by one of the wildebeests.

When she's finished, she turns to the suggestion of specks in the upper section of the painting, the animals farthest away. Everett gave even these dots a certain amount of personal character. One mark will slant to the left, as if it is tossing its head; another will raise its leg in a decidedly reluctant gesture. He used, for the most part, a myriad of grays, touched here and there with a darkening shadow of black. Mary sucks on the end of her brush before dipping it into the paint. She follows his outlines exactly. As she progresses, she feels a gathering of dust in the back of her throat.

She becomes so absorbed that she does not notice the lights in the hall turn off. There is a sudden knock on the glass and she jumps, nearly upsetting the ladder. When she turns, she sees Dr. Fisher, wiping away at the two oval smudges left by the teenager with the inside of his sleeve.

He smiles apologetically. He is perhaps ten years older than she is. Not really old at all. He motions to his watch and Mary nods. She signals that it will take her a few minutes to gather her things, and he indicates that he will wait by the front doors. They have developed this routine over the past few weeks. An evening game of charades.

Mary quickly rinses her brushes in turpentine, packs her paints, and crawls behind an outcropping of rocks through the tiny door leading to the back room. As she comes out into the hall, she pauses for a moment to examine her work. Half of the wall has been completed. The wildebeests fade as they get larger, closer to the leaders of the herd. The painting reminds her of one of her father's, a project he began when he was first diagnosed. She had been away at art school, and it was a shock to come home and find him in bed and the canvas in the living room, a tunneling image unlike anything he'd done before, fading as it grew larger, an inverse explosion.

The paint bag is heavy. It cuts into Mary's shoulder as she walks, her footsteps clicking against the marble. The only light is coming from inside the dioramas, but it is enough for her to find the exit. As she rounds a corner, she glances down the small mammal corridor and sees something large crouching at the end, in the darkness. When she stops, it hesitates for a moment, then moves into the shadows of the reptile room.

Mary feels a rush of fear spread up the backs of her legs and out into her fingertips. She clutches her bag, quickens her pace, and holds her breath until she is through the door. On the other side Dr. Fisher is waiting, his briefcase in hand, his jacket stretched across his tiny, hulking shoulders.

"Something's in there," Mary says. "A dog, maybe, but it was bigger than a dog." She drops her bag on the ground, and then she does something that she never thought she would do. She takes hold of Dr. Fisher's arm with both of her hands and clings to it.

"Are you sure?"

"Yes."

Dr. Fisher walks to the door and Mary shuffles next to him, the fear still in her legs. She is sweating. He opens the door a crack. He sticks his head in.

"Hello?"

"It's not going to answer you," she whispers.

78

"Hit the lights." He is ordering her now. Mary releases his arm and stretches her hand across the wall behind them, flipping the switches. One. Two. Three. The overhead lamps shine. "Where was it?"

"There." She points down the corridor, and that is where Dr. Fisher goes, holding his briefcase in front of him like a shield. Mary watches him cautiously step into the reptile room. She grips the handle of the door, keeping it open just enough, she thinks, looking at it, judging, for Dr. Fisher to slip through if he has to make a run for it. She hears footsteps and glances up. His briefcase is at his side.

"There's nothing there."

"But I'm sure," she begins to say. Mary is still frightened, but she steps tentatively down the corridor to the reptile room. On a table, underneath a thick plate of glass, there are four different piles of eggs. Next to them is a sign that has recently been added, to make the museum more interactive. *Can you guess who will come out of these eggs?* If a button is pushed, the other side of the window lights up and a small preserved group of baby alligators, snakes, turtles, and lizards appears, surrounded by bits of shell. Mary gets on her hands and knees and looks under the table. She stands and searches the corners, the king cobra, the montage of a crocodile swallowing a goat. When she comes out, Dr. Fisher locks the doors behind her. He catches hold of her wrist. Mary is terrified for a moment that he is going to kiss her. Then she realizes he is taking her pulse. He stares at his

79

watch, his lips moving slightly as he counts. She feels nauseated and strangely disappointed.

When Mary gets home, her father is waiting with his glasses on. There are magazines and books on his bed. Except for his emaciated body, he looks like the kind of father she wanted as a teenager, the kind from television, who dispenses advice, stays home every night, and worries about his daughter's virginity.

When she was in high school, her father would disappear. Lock himself into the Chinese noodle factory for days and sometimes weeks, leaving her his checkbook and a small envelope of cash to pay the bills. Mary would order pizza every night and watch television, hating him, then fall asleep with a knife under her pillow because she was afraid of being alone. Eventually her father would emerge and drive her to the factory to show her what he'd done. He always asked the same question: *What does it make you think of?* And Mary would say whatever was in her head at that moment: an orange, a bluebird, a baseball. Sometimes she would still be angry and the images would be different: a rope, a gun, a killer standing in the doorway. He never questioned what she said. He'd make a note with his pencil, and then they would go to a diner and get bacon and eggs and waffles with whipped cream, anything she wanted.

Mary wakes Mercedes, slips her a check at the door.

"How is he?" She hates having to ask this.

"Fine, fine," Mercedes says, but she will not look Mary in the face. She is busy folding the check into a zippered pocket in her bag. "Three shots. Two movements. I washed him. He's clean." Mercedes pulls down the sleeves of her sweater. She does this every day when she leaves. Mary watches her walk down the driveway. Before she gets into her car, she blesses herself.

"I've found the answer," her father says.

"To what?" Mary asks.

"My body."

"Oh, Pop. Not tonight."

"I heard about it on the radio," he says. "This fellow replaces body fluids with plastic—silicone rubber and resin. You last forever."

He hands her the catalog. Inside are photographs of cadavers, partially dissected, posed in the style of great works of art. There is a Mona Lisa in a wig and wraps, her eyelids removed, the muscles of her lips exposed. There is Michelangelo's David split down the middle: one side ligaments and tendons, and the other pure bone.

"How did you get this?"

"I called the artist. He sent it to me."

Mary flips through, page after page. The bodies have been completely deconstructed. She looks at her father's hands resting on the blanket, and thinks of them braiding her hair for school, filling her lunch box, touching her forehead when she had a fever, jumping rope with her, throwing stones for hopscotch.

"I'm not going to go see you in some freaky gallery!"

"It's too late," says her father. "I've already signed the papers."

With the North American mammals, Everett exercised a different set of brushstrokes. Mary notices this first with the mustangs. There is a certain kind of bristle to their coats. She touches the marks on their foreheads—splashes of the same white in the river they are drinking from.

This time, instead of heat, she feels a coolness. As if she has just dipped her hand through the wall into the river. Mary starts to wash away the dirt and notices a smell. It is sweet, like damp hay in the sun. Around the edges of the riverbank, the lines are faded. There are places where the water is seeping out. The strokes are weak, as if Everett had difficulty holding the brush in his hand.

Mary slips into the hall, and tiptoes past Dr. Fisher's office. Whenever a color is too faded, or a figure too small for her to identify, she has been given permission to consult Everett's original notes and sketches, which are kept in the museum library. The room is used only by directors and benefactors. On the shelves are the travel journals of the Roach family, as well as a massive catalog of each exhibit and specimen.

The horses are from North Dakota. Killed over

a hundred years ago. The Roach family kept one in their drawing room. Everett has a small sketch pasted in the catalog, the horse posed between a velvet sofa and a pianoforte. Mary checks the date, and understands why the brushstrokes are different. Michael Everett was dying when he made them.

In one of the travel journals, Mary finds his obituary, clipped from the local news. The print is stained, the paper yellow. He died from consumption soon after completing the dioramas. The Roaches were in Venice at the time. The handwriting in the journal describes the Piazza San Marco as much too hot. There is no mention of Everett. Mary imagines the Roaches' youngest son receiving the news, folded into a letter. Grieving after his lover was already in the ground.

All week her father has been in discussions with the artist who will take his body when he dies. There is a spot open in *The Burghers of Calais*. Rodin is one of her father's favorite sculptors.

"I want to be the man holding the key to the city," he says. "I like the look on his face." He tries it out, lifting his chin, slightly frowning, a crease between his eyebrows, resigned but proud.

Mary watches him practicing in the mirror. There is a photograph of her father, at a similar angle, included in one of his biographies. When the book was published, Mary used it as a reference to fill in her father's secrets. She read about his first tries at painting, his failures. She read about the men in the studio. She read about her mother, an alcoholic he'd met at a party and married against his better judgment. She read about what it had been like for him to hold her as a baby, just after she was born. How large her nose had seemed. How soft the skin was on the bottom of her feet.

When the artist calls, Mary hands her father the phone without speaking. They laugh together. They talk about Goya and William Blake.

"Don't let any collectors buy me," she hears him say. "I want to be in a museum."

When he asks her, she carries the art books down from the study and drops them, crashing, into the pile beside his bed.

"I know you're unhappy about this," her father says. "But it's my body, not yours."

The bell rings, and Mary turns away to open the door. Mercedes is on the welcome mat, rolling up her sleeves.

At the museum, Mary checks over her shoulder. Walks faster. Even when she is inside of the dioramas she does not feel safe. On the ladder, toning the edges of a cloud, she is sure that someone is watching. She turns and sees an elderly couple on the other side of the window.

The old woman's handbag matches the husband's shirt. It is a Hawaiian print, with purple and blue flowers. The old man is wearing sandals. He waves at Mary. His wife is digging through her pocketbook, pulling out her glasses to read the information plaque. On the floor, behind them, is the bear.

The animal has left its pedestal. Its face is round, the snout worn to skin, the eyes made of brown glass. The bear rises on two legs in the marble hallway, close to six feet, swaying a little behind the couple before leaning forward to sniff the old woman's hair.

"Look out!" Mary screams. She gets off the ladder and bangs on the window with both of her hands.

The old woman drops her pocketbook. Her husband freezes, then takes her elbow and begins pulling her away. They both stare at Mary as if she has lost her mind. The bear's attention, meanwhile, has been diverted. The elderly couple makes for the exit, and the bear begins to bounce with its two front paws against the glass.

Mary backs up and knocks over one of the antelopes. With every bounce the window shakes, and she is afraid that it will break. The bear has not changed its expression, but with each push it throws down more weight, until finally one of its legs falls off. The animal drops to three legs and shakes the fourth, horsehair and cotton wadding spilling out of the hole. Mary finds the latch for the trapdoor and slips into the back room.

This is the animal she saw in the corridor last week. She is sure of it. Mary calculates the distance to the exit. She opens the door to the hall a crack. The bear is gone, but Dr. Fisher is there, holding the old woman's handbag.

"What the hell is going on?" he says.

The bear is back in its original position, its face surprised, as if it has just been stumbled upon in the woods. Mary expects to see it breathing, but the body holds still. The only appearance of disorder is the missing leg.

Dr. Fisher puts the strap of the pocketbook over his shoulder and picks up the leg with both hands. He fingers the claws and looks at Mary carefully. His eyes are the same brown as the bear's. "Did you do this?"

"No," Mary says. "It fell off."

"We can't have that," Dr. Fisher says, frowning. He takes off his jacket, folds it and sets it aside with the purse. A small sewing kit appears from his back pocket. He chooses a needle and thread and looks for a way to reattach the leg. "I'll need you to get hold around the front and lift."

Mary pauses. She is afraid to get close. Dr. Fisher crouches, waiting. She steps onto the pedestal, her sneakers hovering near the edge. There is a slight give as Mary reaches around the body. The weight is similar to her father's after his first operation, when she had to boost him onto the toilet. He could barely stand for her to do this. After he finished she would pat her father's arm, meaning, *I would do anything for you,* and this is what Mary finds herself thinking as she touches the bear's fur. The animal stays frozen, impassive as a table. There is a smell coming from its mouth.

"My mother taught me how to sew before she

died," Dr. Fisher says. "She was afraid I'd never get married." He breaks off a length of string with his teeth.

Mary waits for the bear to move in her arms. She watches Dr. Fisher sew. The back of his neck is shaved in a clear, straight line. "My father doesn't believe in marriage."

"Wasn't he married to your mother?"

"Yes," Mary says. "It was a mistake."

"So you're off the idea?"

"Not really," she says. "But I can't imagine being that close to anyone." He looks up, studying her face, and she blushes. The leg dangles loosely from the bear's shoulder.

"You can let him down now."

Mary bends, slowly releasing the weight to the floor. When she takes her hands away, they are covered with dust.

Her father insists on coming to see the finished paintings. "This is your first opening," he says. "I'm not going to miss it."

There is a lot of preparation. Through Mercedes, she borrows a wheelchair from the hospice center. She gets a van with a ramp from one of the guards at the museum. Her father wants to wear a suit. Mary helps him get dressed. His body has shrunk. The pants and jacket seem made for a different man. She ties an ascot loosely around his throat. She combs what is left of his hair.

"I want the windows open," he says in the van.

She rolls them all the way down. Mary is already feeling exhausted, but her father seems refreshed. As she drives, she looks in the rearview mirror and watches him lean his face into the breeze, the way a dog might.

Dr. Fisher is waiting for them at the handicapped entrance. He insists on giving a tour. Mary feels awkward introducing the men, but her father is friendly. He asks questions about the collection and its history. When Dr. Fisher spends twenty minutes describing the life cycle of a turtle, her father bats his eyes before spitting a wad of phlegm into his handkerchief.

At last they turn in to the exhibition hall. Dr. Fisher has lost some of his steam and Mary is thankful for the silence. She wheels her father up to a set of camels, dromedary and Bactrian.

"Oh, sweetheart," her father says. "Just look at that sand."

Mary suddenly feels choked. She is not prepared for compliments, although she is proud of the texture and light she has given back to the dunes. She tries to deflect the attention, insists that the pyramids in the background are crude, but her father points out that it was Everett's choice to include them, not hers.

"Makes the animals look a little shabby." He tries to wink, but instead closes both of his eyes.

Mary is unsure if her restoration has drawn her father's interest, or Everett's paintings underneath. She has copied strokes, matched colors, followed lines, given trees and animals dimension and shade, but none of this is truly hers.

They wheel past the migration of the wildebeests.

"I'd like to try my hand at this," her father says. He knocks on the glass. "It's like a time capsule."

Mary tries to imagine him well enough. The last painting he did was a self-portrait, a ghostly rendering in blues and blacks. He'd tacked it to the wall of their living room and then said he was going to bed. When she opened the door to his room, he had the covers pulled up to his chin. His face looked frightened. She suggested they go to the hospital, and he did not say no, and it was then that she first felt it—the hollowness of what her life would be without him.

Before he got sick, his hands had always been covered with paint. Knuckles and fingernails stained purple and red. When she was a girl, he showed her how to mix colors by blending them right on his skin. The backs of his hands and the space above his wrist. He used his entire palette to create one tone. He told her there was no true white.

They stop in front of the bear, still posed with its head lifted, the leg precariously askew. Her father is interested in the teeth. Mary pushes the wheelchair up to the mouth and recognizes the smell coming from it. The same combination of mildew and rot has been on her father's body for weeks. When she washes his arms and legs and neck, even the sponge comes away with the smell, even the water. Mary grabs hold of her father's shoulders as if he might be taken right from the wheelchair, and pushes him away, down the hall.

"I wasn't finished," her father is saying.

They are reflected in each diorama as they pass. She can see her father waving, trying to get her to stop. If she could, she would preserve him in a window of his own. Paint the Chinese letters of the noodle factory across the wall. Arrange the tubes of oils, spread the brushes, hang the works in progress, prop the bed up in the corner. She wants to keep every part of him for herself. She wants to scream.

Dr. Fisher hurries to keep up. The bear, he says, has no natural predators. It can run up to thirty miles per hour. He looks distraught and tries to catch her eye. He wants to know if he has done something wrong.

Mary turns quickly and glances back. The dioramas are lit up like show lights, and on the pedestal, where the bear should be, is nothing at all. She feels the urge to run. To push her father straight through the emergency exit doors. Instead she focuses on Dr. Fisher's voice. He says that bears hibernate for six months at a time. Their heartbeats drop. They barely breathe, but they are still alive. Mary imagines waking from a sleep like this. The hunger sure to follow. She can sense the animal, with its sad stitching, stumbling behind them.

SLIM'S LAST RIDE

I don't know why Rick thought the rabbit could fly. He knows he can't. He knows I can't. He must have thought something would keep it from falling, or he never would have let it go.

When Rick's father came by and gave him that rabbit, I hadn't heard from him in three years. Boo for three years and suddenly he's on my front porch in a pair of worn-out boots, saying he's got a present for his boy. Rap, rap, rap. I put my hand on the screen door between us and held it closed. I hadn't washed my hair for days.

I told him to leave it on the steps. He put the cage down and I could see something white moving around inside. I wondered if he still had the keys to my house that I'd made for him. I didn't get mad until he started to walk away.

"Well," I shouted after him. "How do I look?"

"Good," he said, but he didn't turn around. "You look good."

Rick said he'd call it Slim.

My son liked to dress Slim in his clothes and carry him around, like a doll or a lucky charm. At first I thought this was cute, but then that rabbit started getting all fat and almost as big as Rick, and I got a little scared. Slim had nails and teeth and could do some damage. I kept an eye on him, but he wasn't any trouble. He always hung limp in Rick's arms, his big back thumper legs spread out and relaxed like he was waiting on something.

Rick made him a home in the backyard with an old lobster trap he'd dragged up from the beach. Rick's nine. He's resourceful. The wood was prickly and gray. When I'd get back from work, I'd find Rick out in the yard, adding something new to Slim's hutch.

"Is this all you do after school till I come home?" I asked him. I pointed to our old push lawn mower leaning against the side of the house. "Why isn't the grass cut? Where's my turkey dinner?" Rick smiled—he knows when I'm joking—and worked on sticking a pile of speckled pebbles in a row, one by one, to a thin white line of Elmer's glue. I dipped my finger in it. Sticky, sticky. Then I slid my hand between the bars of the cage and wiped it on the rabbit's fur. Silky. Silky Slim.

I bought one of those hamster water bottles. It hangs upside down and has a tiny metal ball in its throat that keeps the water from flowing out when someone isn't licking. I bought a big bag of alfalfa pellets. Each night I poured the rabbit food into the cover of an old mayonnaise jar. Rick would get so excited he'd spill most of the pellets before he made it over to the cage, and he'd have to come back and fill the lid again. I'd never get mad; I'd just pour some more. That's the kind of mother I am.

Slim became a problem when he started wearing Rick's underwear. I found out when I did the laundry. When I go to the Laundromat, I always count my clothes. I keep a list, and I write things down as I put them in the washer—four T-shirts, one skirt, twenty-seven socks, three jeans, six pillowcases, thirteen pairs of underwear, two towels. Then I check them off the list as I pull them out, wet and stiff from the spin cycle so I always leave with what I came in with. I don't like to lose things.

It was Saturday and I was waiting for the washer to stop. I didn't mind waiting. It was my time. I'd paid my quarters. I could see a reflection of a face in the little round window of the washer. I stuck my tongue out to make sure it was me.

The red light went off and I pulled my wheelie basket around, picked up my notepad, and started to count and check. I got as far as the third T-shirt, and I noticed that there was some brown stuff in my laundry. There were dark smudges on the clothes I had just washed. There were teeny caca marks on my permanent-press, extra-soak, sixteen-quarter full load. I picked up a pair of Superman Underoos, and they were full of soggy rabbit doots.

I took a deep breath. My skin was stretching, getting tighter, and I got this light, airy feeling as if I was about to lift right off the floor. I dumped the doots into the garbage, ran another sixteen-quarter full load, and when I got home, I found Rick outside and I jammed those dooty-stained shorts on his head. My hands grabbed on to his shoulders and shook, shook, shook him until his face turned white and I felt the weight of me coming back down again.

When I was done, Rick slipped to the ground and pulled the Underoos over his face. I watched his breath make the little Superman rise and fall, and sat next to him on the grass. I ran my fingers over the blades, held on, and pulled out a clump of dirt. I dangled it over Superman's face and moved it back and forth until the grains hanging on to the roots began to sprinkle.

"Look," I said. "It's pixie dust." Rick rolled to his side and peeked at me through one of the leg holes. I gave him a smile. Then I stood up, threw the clump away, and started hanging the clothes on the line.

I never use the dryers at the Laundromat. Why should I pay for something that my garments can do perfectly well on their own? Having my laundry spread out in front of me on the clothesline makes me feel calm inside. I can see where everything is.

The first time Rick threw Slim out the window, I came home from work and found the cage empty. I got this funny "something's wrong" feeling, and I knew I was right when I walked into the kitchen. The rabbit was in the sink and Rick was under the table.

"What did you do?" I said. I threw down my pocketbook, and Rick grabbed his T-shirt and pulled the front of it over his head. He does this when he knows he's done something wrong. He doesn't have to get caught, either. Sometimes I'll be kicking back with a cigarette, maybe a glass of red wine, and Rick will walk into the room with his shirt pulled tight over his head like some kind of headless horseman, his arms hanging limp out of the sleeves on either side, his belly bare. In the room, out of the room. Not a word. In, out. It's a sign. Then all I have to do is follow his trail back where he's come from and I'll always find something wrong.

Slim was scratching and clamoring around in the sink. His nails made tiny tinny noises on the metal like something awful. Rat-tat-tat-tat-tat. He was shaking all over, and one of his big back legs was stuck out sideways and dragging behind him.

Rick's voice came from underneath the table. He told me that Slim fell and now he wouldn't stop biting.

"That's because his leg is broken," I said. "His leg looks like it's about to fall off." I crouched down. I could see Rick's little white belly. His chest was shivering in and out, and I realized he was crying.

"Come here," I said. Rick crawled over to me. I scooped him up like a baby and pulled him onto my lap. I took his shirt off his head and tucked it into his pants. I held his face in my hands and rubbed the tears off his cheeks with the tips of my thumbs. "Watch," I said. "I'll make it better."

Slim was squealing, cheep-cheep sounds like a bird. I put on some thick yellow rubber gloves I had under the sink—I wasn't going to let that rabbit bite me—and after much struggle-struggle I wrapped up Slim's leg tight between two pencils with some electrical tape. "Now, no more hopping for a week," I said sternly, and Rick laughed.

Then I did all the right things. I took Rick into the bathroom and washed his face with a cool wet washcloth. I found a comb in the medicine cabinet and wet that too and combed his hair down straight. I gave him a pinch to make him laugh again. "Who loves you?" I said. And he said, "You do."

I make spare keys at the True Value Hardware store downtown. I'm fast. People come to me with worried faces. They look me up and down. It makes them nervous to give up their keys, even for a minute, but they hand them over. And I think, *What do they see when they look at me?* I hold the pieces of metal in my hand and hear the locks turn, the doors opening, as I take them off their owners' key chains. I point to the clock on the wall. "Time me," I say.

I take their keys, square and round, long and short, and find a match from the wallboard behind me. Hundreds of key types hang from tiny hooks, all uncut. No teeth. They won't let you into anything. I grab the key and clamp it in my machine. Tuck, tuck the spare into the cutting space, put my goggles on, and start the motor. The wheel spins fast and hard and makes sounds like teeth together on metal. Grind, in, out. Unclamp, shift. Clamp. Grind, in, out. Unclamp, shift. Clamp. Grind, in, out. Unclamp. Ting. "Be careful," I say. "It's hot."

I was making a delivery when I met Rick's dad. Fifty-three keys to a high-wire fence at an amusement park based on farm animals. I drove up to Farmland and they welcomed me inside. It was their semiannual county fair day, and Rick's dad was demonstrating how a tractor works. When I saw him dragging that chained-up ton of cement blocks with his machine, the wheels churning and the mud flying up in his face, and the way he turned and smiled into it like it was a sweet spring rain, I knew it was love. Two county fairs later I was pregnant.

I marked the nights he stayed at my house with Xs on the calendar. I made him keys so he could stop by when he wanted. After the baby the times he showed grew apart—Mondays and Tuesdays went to every other Friday and then one Sunday a month. When I didn't have a day to X on, I started to X on myself. Little lines down the length of my nose, crosshatches on my cheekbones. I tried to see how I looked in the shine of the toaster, then tiptoed over to Rick's crib and peeped in.

He slept with his arms covering his head. He always seemed to be ducking.

Rick's dad left Farmland and decided he wanted to work his way across the country. He took the keys I'd made, and late at night I listened for the sound of them sliding into my locks. He sent me one letter, five postcards, and a melon from California. Then three years of boo. Then Slim.

I was in my bedroom when I heard the thump. It was a heavy, solid thump with a clang at the end, and I thought, *Now, that's something*. I always know when it's something. I heard Rick running down the stairs past my room and out the back door. I went to the closet and put on a yellow sweater. Yellow is my favorite color. Sunny-side up, I say.

I raised the shade. Rick had his shirt off and was covering something with it on the ground by the lawn mower. A sleeve was caught on one of the blades. I watched Rick unhook it with his fingertips, wipe it on one of the big rubber wheels, and tuck it underneath the pile. The sun was bright on his little white shoulders. I opened the window and stuck my head out.

"Hey!" I said. "I just washed that, you know! So don't go throwing it on the ground. Pick it up. Pick it up," I said. "I'm not your trash lady!" I have to remind Rick so he doesn't forget these things. I say, I'm not your washerwoman, I'm not your wife, I'm not your fairy godmother.

Rick stood when he heard my voice and put his arms out straight in the air. He looked like Frankenstein. Frankenstein kid. His shirt was still on the ground, tucked in front of the lawn mower blades. There was a lump there underneath it. I could tell he was trying to keep me from seeing something.

"Move!" I said. "You're not fooling anyone standing there like an idiot. There's nothing wrong with you." Rick didn't even blink. He looked frozen. His mouth was open, and I could see his little tongue in there. I took a breath down deep in my chest and screamed, half 'cause I was getting mad, half 'cause I thought I might scare him out of it.

"MOOOOOOOVE!"

And just then that little bundle gave a shoulder and a hop, hop, hop. If you could call it a hop. It was more like a lurch. Like a drag. It rolled off from the lawn mower and started across the grass. "Up, up, and away!" said Rick. I stood there at the window, watching Rick shouting and that lump scooting along, and I started to laugh. It was funny.

I went downstairs. I sent the screen door swinging behind me—creak-slam! Put, put, put, down the back steps and outside. Rick had his eyes fixed on the shirt flopping away. I started after it. I made a show.

"Come back here, shirt!" I said. "You think you're getting away from me?" It tried to fake me out with a zigzag, but I caught it easy and put my foot on it. I held it fast, picked up a side, and started shaking it. "Get!" I said. The little shirt un-rolled, and out came Slim in what seemed like pieces, a sticky mess all white and red.

It looked as though someone had sliced him right down the side, from the back of his ear to the front curve of his thumper leg. He moved and I noticed that the skin wasn't just cut. A whole piece had been peeled away, and I could see the wet pink sponge of muscle underneath the blood. I poked him with my foot and he slumped over. Part of his little front leg was gone.

I turned around and looked at Rick. He was in the same spot and his arms were reaching out at me. Frankenstein kid. I walked over with his grass-stained, rabbit blood shirt in my hand and kneeled in front of him. He let his arms down, let them rest on my shoulders, and when I pulled him close to me, I felt them give a squeeze.

"Let go," I said, and his arms dropped. He looked at my right shoulder, then at my left shoulder, then over at Slim on the grass. "Look at me!" I said, and I grabbed his chin and lifted it to my face. It was his father's chin—longish, with a slight dimple. I pressed my thumb into it hard.

I made Rick put on his shirt. I pushed the collar down, and when his head came through, it was streaked a rusty red. I pulled the shirt over his belly. The cloth was wet and cold, and when I saw the blood caking into my knuckles, I knew it would never wash out. Rick bent his elbow and pushed his arm through a sleeve, and something flew out the cuff onto the lawn.

At first I thought it was a piece of wadded-up tissue. Rick was always carrying them around, balled in his fist. When I changed his bed, I'd find shreds of them in the sheets, as if he'd been up all night, tearing them to bits—but this wasn't a tissue. It was Slim's front leg.

We both looked at it for a while. A tiny white thing on the grass. Then I thought of something. "Pick it up," I said. Rick stared at the ground. "Do it," I said. Rick took the front of his shirt and tried to put it over his head. "No." I said. I pulled it back down. "No more hiding. Hiding is for babies. Now, I want you to pick that up and get rid of it. It's time you learned to clean up after yourself. I'll take care of the rest."

I left him out there with Slim's leg and went inside to pull those yellow gloves out from under the sink again. No bites for me! Then I went back outside. Rick had picked up the little piece of rabbit and was pressing the tip of his finger against the paw pads.

I took a towel off the clothesline and put the clothespins in my pocket. I walked over to the rabbit, scooped it all up, and brought it inside.

Slim had stopped moving. I put the towel down carefully in the sink and opened it up to take a look at him. I thought he might be dead, but as soon as I touched his shoulder, he started scrambling, clawing at me. I held him tight. He wasn't going anywhere.

I scrounged some codeine out of the medicine cabinet, ground it up, and put it in Slim's water. That helped. I held his glass feeder like it was a baby's bottle. When he calmed down enough, I tied his little stump tight.

I went to look for a needle. I got some dental floss out of the medicine cabinet—mint. When I got back to the kitchen, Slim was out cold. I pulled the pieces of his skin together till they overlapped and clipped them with a clothespin from my pocket. I ran the end of a piece of floss through my lips to thread the needle—mint!—and tied the end in a knot. When I pushed the point through his skin, there was a tiny pop, and then it slid through nicely. I sewed up his side. I used a cross-stitch. I'm no seamstress, but it didn't look bad.

Before Rick's father left to travel the country, he called me and said he wanted to see his son. He took us to Farmland's company picnic. We followed the trails in and out of the World of Poultry, and around the Land of Grazing. Rick's dad unlocked the gates with the keys I'd made and let us pet the animals. We got to go on the rides for free.

We stopped by Farmland's learning center. Kids could study different animals' anatomy there, or act out the animals' jobs on the farm. In one area they had special goggles, like viewfinders, and if you looked into them you could see how a cow sees or see how a duck sees. They fixed the insides with mirrors to take out the color if the animal didn't see in color, or block out the sides if the animal could only see straight ahead, or fragment it if the animal could only see pieces of things.

I picked up a pair of those animal viewfinders and put them on. I looked at Rick's father. *This is how a dog sees you,* I thought. *This is how a chicken sees you.* I turned to where Rick was and saw nothing. Sky. I looked down to find him, and there were my feet on the ground. They seemed far away. I had to move them to make sure they were real. Shuffle step. Point my toe. Tap, tap the ground in front of me to make sure that was real too.

The last time Rick threw Slim out the window, I was in the yard, pinning sheets to the line. The wind was catching them, snapping them, trying to pull them from my fingers, and I had to hold on hard to keep them from blowing across the lawn. I had one pillowcase left. Two pins in my hand. I heard Rick shout, "Up, up, and away," and when I looked, he threw Slim out the third-story window.

Slim's fur was flowing all around him. His ears were back and his body was spread out, the skin on his sides flapping like it was trying to catch air. Rick had tied a little cape around his neck, and I realized that it was an old diaper I'd been using as a dishrag. I watched Slim come right at my face and I thought, *That stupid rabbit, he isn't even looking down.*

Slim wasn't much of a rabbit anymore. He'd been hobbling around on three legs for a couple of weeks. We'd moved his cage inside to help him heal, but it hadn't done much good. He hadn't been eating, just sucking down codeine and carrot juice, and his skin had started hanging on his bones. I watched him coming at me, and I knew this was his last ride.

I wondered if Slim knew what was happening. If he was waving his little stump in the air in anticipation of the smack, or if that was too much for his little brain to remember. Maybe this felt new to him, falling from Rick to me. Maybe he was having a good time.

HIT MAN OF THE YEAR

Ambruzzo came out fists first. He was wet and blue, and his grandmother, in a panic, wrapped him in her apron and set him in the oven to keep him warm. As she bent and peered at her grandson nestled between the metal racks, Nonna felt an eerie dread that stayed with her even after she saw the color rise in his skin, like one, she would later say, coming back from the dead. She said a Hail Mary quickly under her breath and used the mitts to pull him out of the oven.

Earlier that afternoon, Nonna had found her daughter in the back room of the family bakery, dusted in flour and marking a rolling pin with her teeth.

"I'm pregnant," said Sylvia, her voice like the growl of a dog. She'd always been a plump girl and her mother hadn't noticed the changes. Later Nonna would remember them all, but for now she made space on the mixing table; she pushed the sugar, salt, and butter aside, then helped her daughter up.

When the contractions came closer, she asked her *Who*, but Sylvia wouldn't answer. Not in the

109

white heat of muscle tearing. Not in the timed pool of numbness in between. Not when a piece of her broke loose inside and Sylvia slid with the blood away from her body, across the table, till there was nothing left and she was gone.

Nonna buried her daughter and brought up the baby in the bakery. She watched his brown curls grow, his blue eyes darken, and looked for signs of the man who had killed her little girl. She watched for him in the streets, on Sundays in church, and at the festivals: San Gennaro, San Antonio, Corpus Christi. She was a patient woman. She bided her time, filled and measured it like flour and piled it around her heart.

She decided to name the baby after her great-grandfather, whom she had only seen once in a blurred photograph, a splash of white obscuring his face—the glare of the sun, or perhaps a mustache. Ambruzzo Spagnetti was a quiet child. He grew to be clever, and his grandmother began to depend on him.

Mrs. Fabrizio liked to wear tropical wraparound dresses with shoes dyed to match. They were all the same style—a high heel that clicked, and a strap around the ankle. Ambruzzo looked forward to seeing the shoes each week. He was ten years old and loved the way a ten-year-old does: unflinchingly, and with an eye for color. But Nonna didn't trust her, didn't like the way her long black hair always hung loose around her shoulders. When

Mrs. Fabrizio placed her order, she would lean across the counter, and Nonna always felt she was trying to see inside the change drawer.

On a bright Saturday afternoon Ambruzzo delivered a dozen rolls to Mrs. Fabrizio's apartment. She thanked him and placed the rolls inside a suitcase laid out on her kitchen table.

It was a two-room apartment. The couch was pulled open into a bed. The sheets were pushed down and Ambruzzo saw there was a stain in the center of the mattress. One of the pillows had been ripped and there were feathers on the floor, piled on a table, strewn across a lamp shade. Mrs. Fabrizio handed Ambruzzo a bag full of her shoes and asked him to walk her to the bus station.

On the way she told Ambruzzo to look behind them, and he would say with his usual curtness that no one's there, or it's only some kids, or it's only Mrs. Rondo or Larry Pulcheck with his dog. She told him he was good and Ambruzzo felt his cheeks warm. He looked down. Mrs. Fabrizio wasn't wearing any stockings. Her legs were covered with a fine, dark stubble.

As he waited outside the station for Mrs. Fabrizio to buy her ticket, Ambruzzo was approached by a striped suit. The man in the suit tapped the boy on the shoulder, then kept his hand there and squeezed.

"She leaving?" he asked. Ambruzzo shook his head, and the suit laughed loudly, HA, then HA again. Some spit came out of his mouth and

Ambruzzo felt it on his forehead. The man reached inside his coat pocket and slipped a coin into Ambruzzo's hand. It was a Buffalo nickel. "I'm not here." He walked around the bus parked in front till Ambruzzo couldn't see him anymore.

Before Mrs. Fabrizio got on the bus, she handed Ambruzzo a pair of shoes and told him to give them to his grandmother. They were a bright canary yellow. Ambruzzo imagined Nonna trying to push her callused toes inside and decided to keep the shoes for himself. He held on to the ankle straps as Mrs. Fabrizio climbed the stairs. He waved good-bye. Then he walked carefully to the end of the bus and peered around the corner.

The man in the striped suit was on the other side, crouching in the street. He was holding a switchblade. A car sped closely by him, and he pressed up against the wheels of the bus.

Ambruzzo hoped that Mrs. Fabrizio would not choose a seat with a window on that side. That she would not arrange her packages overhead, introduce herself to her traveling companion, and glance out the window to see Ambruzzo shove the man under the wheels of the nonstop express to Port Authority. As the weight pushed free of his hands, Ambruzzo sensed movement behind him. He felt the heat on his neck, smelled the exhaust and knew that he was on his way.

Ambruzzo had a gift. Martin Spordonza had seen this long ago, when Ambruzzo was known as the silent child. Customers in the bakery said his quietness was a blessing, but Nonna felt something unnatural about it; she knew it was unlucky when a baby didn't cry. Martin Spordonza held his thin, fragile box of cannoli and peered into the cradle Nonna kept on the racks between the sweet rolls and the pizzelles. Ambruzzo returned his look like a pool of water—indifferent and cool—and Martin had a vision of his future business. He decided to get a hold on Ambruzzo and, when the time was right, launch him in the Spordonza family like the paper ships he'd sailed as a boy.

Martin Spordonza was ten years old when Nonna began running Spagnetti's Bakery on her own. He had recently discovered the importance of his family's name in the neighborhood and was starting to test himself against it. Early one morning he smashed a side window of the bakery, climbed through, and used a baseball bat to break open the register. As he left the store, Martin looped a dozen brossadellas along the bat like Christmas wreaths. He handed them to strangers on his way to school, accepting their thanks with an authoritative nod.

Later that day, Nonna caught him on the street. She took his bat, and as Martin and his friends watched, she smashed it against a fire hydrant until it splintered into pieces. The children stood by, quietly expectant, as Nonna caught her breath. They scattered when she started slapping. Martin's ears rang all the way to the priest, where he was forced to confess, then Nonna dragged him home, her fingernails raking his arm.

Even after his father chided him for robbing a widow and pledged Nonna family protection for life, Martin refused to apologize. For this Nonna continued to cuff him when he came into the bakery or when she saw him on the street. These blows slowly won Martin's admiration and respect. He was impressed by Nonna's fearlessness and sought to rectify his standing with her. Years later, he continued to try.

Ambruzzo's involvement with the Spordonza family began with deliveries on his route for the bakery and soon became a full-time after-school job of hustling. Martin was careful to keep the boy's work within a strict time frame set by Nonna. Ambruzzo's duties were not to interfere with his studies, force him to miss a meal, or prevent him from tending the bread on Sunday mornings.

Ambruzzo's grandmother was a practical woman. She had been sent to America by her parents when she was sixteen years old. At night, while she tried to sleep in the small attic room of the family she cleaned for, she had listened to the wind rattle the windows like teeth and imagined the place overflowing with her children and her children's children. She'd stuff the room with her descendants, contemplate each nose, chin, and earlobe, and think of names—first names, middle names, confirmation names—an endless stream of words to fill the cold, thin, empty air.

Her chance at a family came while she was shopping for bread. The baker was a bachelor, a man who'd lived with his mother—a mother who had died the week before. Nonna gave him one of the sweet sausages she'd just bought at the butcher's. On the next visit, she offered to wash his shirts. Another month and they were married and she was suddenly full, with a man and a baby and a home. Later, when she laid her husband in the ground and then her daughter, she had to find something to fill up the space: cookies, rolls, and star bread on Sundays. She poured sugar and measured salt.

Nonna watched with a mixture of regret and relief as her grandson left for Spordonza's each day. She had seen his fate coming in a cup of Earl Grey. The tea had tumbled into her saucer and shown an unnatural equanimity. She had already been witness to his effortless composure: a hand burnt on the oven, a broken arm from a fall off a bicycle, a severe case of chicken pox endured without a whimper. The wet brown leaves tracked across her good china and filled in Ambruzzo's future.

When he was fifteen Ambruzzo fell in love. Her name was Amy Stackenfrach, a redhead who sat diagonally across from him in his third-period U.S. history class. She had a mole at the base of her neck in the shape of a twisted oval. It looked like a tiny, tiny mouth, and the longer Ambruzzo stared at it, the more he felt the urge to put his finger there.

He often caught glimpses of her doodles—furious drawings in dark blue pen. One day, in heavy lines that left grooves on the paper, he made out the head and shoulders of an American prairie buffalo. Ambruzzo slid a finger into his pocket, touching the edge of the nickel that the man in the striped suit had given him. He was in the habit of bringing it everywhere—in his jacket, his shoe, his sock—and tracing the indentation of the buffalo with his fingers. Ambruzzo learned how to roll the nickel back and forth across his knuckles, a sliding silvery fish. During Mass, he'd feel it in the pocket of his dress shirt, rising and falling. It rested lightly there, as soft as the Communion wafer on his tongue.

He still had Mrs. Fabrizio's shoes, hidden in the corner of his closet. When he was younger, he'd take one out and sleep with it, the heel tucked under his chin. Lately, he'd been pulling it out again, brushing the smooth yellow satin down his chest and across the soft insides of his arms late at night when he couldn't sleep.

Stampede, his history teacher was saying, *stampede.* She pulled down maps of the prairie nations. She used a pointer to illustrate movement. She asked Ambruzzo to name the tribes. He knew three: Apache, Chippewa, and Sioux.

After school, he followed Amy Stackenfrach home. He waited in the bushes until dark, then went through her mailbox, eyeing Mr. Stackenfrach's letters and Mrs. Stackenfrach's catalogs and magazines. He pocketed the phone bill and climbed a maple tree in the front yard. He watched Amy do her homework on the dining room table, and when she scratched her nose, he touched his too, pretending it was a signal between them.

The next day he asked her what she knew about buffalo.

"They're really called bison," Amy said. "The Indians used their tongues for hairbrushes."

Ambruzzo said that was cool. He asked if he could buy her a milk shake. At the Dairy Queen, he showed her his nickel.

"Oh," she said. "Neat." She took it from his hand, licked it, and stuck it to her eyelid. Ambruzzo watched it shining there and felt his stomach drop. He listened to her explain how to turn hides into tipis, horns into powder flasks, lower intestines into tobacco pouches.

"Do you smoke?" she asked him.

Ambruzzo shook his head.

"You should. You look like a gangster."

Ambruzzo glanced at his hands. They were wide, the fingers short and stubby.

He began to go regularly through the Stackenfrach trash barrels. He discovered that Amy's father had a penchant for stout, that Amy's mother paid the bills, and that the entire family relied heavily on Dixie cups. He also found scraps of paper covered with dark blue pen, and on them, the beginnings of love letters scratched out.

Dear Joe:
  You don't know me, but I know you.

Dear Charlie:
  Hello there.

Dear Mark:
  This might seem strange, but

Ambruzzo read them over and over. He crossed out the names and tried putting in his own. It looked odd, and his crippled handwriting next to her clean lines made him feel like a failure. He drew a list, cross-referenced it with the school roster. Joe and Mark transferred to other districts. Charlie dropped out and joined the Navy.

After high school, the Spordonza family sent Ambruzzo to Bologna for training. He wrote letters to Amy Stackenfrach to which she at first politely replied from her small private college on the East Coast. He talked about the weather and not about what he was learning: How to suffocate. How to follow people. How to shoot things from far away. How to blend into a passing crowd, the words on a billboard, a breeze moving slowly through the leaves of a tree.

Ambruzzo enjoyed rereading Amy's letters. Sometimes she would pen her responses along the edges of the same pieces of paper he had so carefully chosen, folded, and sent to her. Amy wrote about her art teacher, about the smell from the river, about the Watusi and the boys she was dating. Ambruzzo asked their names, where they lived, if he could come to visit. She returned his next letter unopened with a note along the seal: *Please don't write anymore.*

In some ways this made life easier. It was as if a small hole in the ice of him had suddenly closed up, and now he was a solid, blank surface. Ambruzzo rose to the top of his class. He was put in specialized training—electrocution to poison darts. Nonna mailed him a prayer card of Saint Anthony of Padua. *I am fine,* she wrote. *The bread is fine too. When do you come home? Where is my family?* Ambruzzo kept Saint Anthony on his bedside table and tried to think of things he wanted.

His first professional hit was a minor one: Louie Morona, a class-D welsher who'd turned state's evidence and entered the witness protection program. Ambruzzo trailed him from New York to Hayward, Wisconsin. He found Louie on the Ojibwa Indian reservation, attempting to pass as a Native American.

Ambruzzo used his belt to strangle Louie in the cornfield behind the casino. The belt was new; Ambruzzo had bought it that day in downtown Hayward. It was a good length and fit nicely in the space between Louie Morona's Adam's apple and the base of his throat. Ambruzzo cut off Louie's fingers and toes, shot him once in the face, and dumped his body in Lake Courte Oreilles. On his way out of town, he stopped by the post office and overnighted Louie's digits to Martin Spordonza.

As he traveled back east, Ambruzzo thought of two things: the canary yellow shoes of Mrs. Fabrizio, waiting for him in his closet at home, and Louie Morona's feet with the toes cut off—how demure they had seemed.

He began to wear suits. Double-breasted, with matching vests and wide ties. Nonna told him he looked handsome. She was pleased to have him home with her again. In the morning Ambruzzo tended the mixers and the ovens. Nonna worked till noon, then closed for lunch: warm bread, tomatoes, and hard strong cheese. In the afternoons she gossiped and ran the cash register, and Ambruzzo met Spordonza at the Sons of Italy.

Martin told him his new assignment over cappuccinos and a bag of M&M's. He separated the candies into piles: dark brown, light brown, orange, yellow, and green. Each color designating a level of power. Dark brown were soldiers. Yellow, consiglieri. Martin slid a green candy across the table and Ambruzzo knew who was next: Rocco Briolli.

Rocco had been the head of the Briolli family for twenty-five years, controlling the flow, distribution, and sale of all produce in New York City. Eight million people needed their fruits and vegetables. Martin Spordonza wanted his share of the business.

Ambruzzo spent a month preparing. He tracked Briolli's movements, his routines and pastimes, and found the perfect opening: a benefit for the restoration of North American mammal dioramas at the Museum of Natural History. Briolli, an amateur taxidermist, enjoyed strolling through the re-created scenes. He was a dedicated sponsor, on the board of trustees, and personally sent out the invitations.

A band was set in front of the mountain lions. The bar next to the wapiti. Hors d'oeuvres circulated in the small mammals corridor by the collared peccary and the red-backed vole. Ambruzzo wore a tuxedo. He sat on a bench in front of the bison. There were five of them behind the glass. Their coats looked dusty; the painted background depicting the rest of the herd was cracked and yellowing with age. Ambuzzo was amazed at their size and, despite their circumstances, the power they projected.

Yesterday he secretly installed an automatic weapon inside the head of the Alaskan brown bear, armed with a remote-control release. The control was now in his left jacket pocket, and as Rocco Briolli paused in front of the glass to point out the detailing that needed some work—the lips should be repainted, the bear was missing several claws—Ambruzzo sprayed him with a quick, short burst of fire.

The glass between the bear and the party guests shattered. Two bullets pierced Rocco's chest and another whizzed through his trachea. He staggered, blood rushed from the hole in his neck, and Ambruzzo sprayed again, this time blowing away a good portion of Rocco's skull while bringing down two Wall Street executives and a tenor for the New York Metropolitan Opera. Briolli's men returned fire on the bear, detaching the front legs and ripping into the stuffing. The bear collapsed onto its mate. Broken glass covered the marble floor, and the patrons rushed for the exits, seeking cover in Africa and the Pacific Islands. Ambruzzo took a glass of champagne and walked steadily up the stairs and past the dinosaurs on his way out. He regretted the tenor.

Waiting for nightfall underneath the low branches of a forsythia, Ambruzzo began to question his existence. He trained his scope on a young man and woman, light brown and orange M&M's. They were having a picnic. A bottle of wine was propped between the young woman's legs. There were sandwiches on rye and small jars of honey mustard and green tomato chutney on the blanket.

When Ambruzzo returned from training camp in Bologna, he asked Nonna what it was like to love. She was wearing slippers and rolling gnocchi for dinner.

"My hands are old," she said. She held them out; her forearms were thick and covered with moles. She turned them over. She sighed. "Love is like dying, like saying good-bye."

Sometimes he will think about the person he is killing. Sometimes he will not.

The young couple spread cheese onto crackers. Ambruzzo watched the girl wipe crumbs off the young man's lips with a piece of napkin. He was amazed that grown people did this for each other. It was common, he realized; he had seen it through his scope at other times: a smudge of chocolate, a dribble of tomato sauce, a mustache of Hawaiian Punch.

He waited for them to finish dessert. Seedless grapes and Chips Ahoy! cookies. The young woman began to pack the cooler. He shot her as she was closing a Ziploc baggie. He could see pickle juice spilling over the lawn. She crumpled so quietly that the young man, shaking out their blanket, did not notice. Ambruzzo got him before he did.

The Spordonza family was booming. Martin congratulated himself on his foresight and gave Ambruzzo a plaque engraved HIT MAN OF THE YEAR. He considered moving to Montana and taking up fly-fishing. With the fiscal goal of his retirement on the horizon, Spordonza slipped Ambruzzo another green M&M.

Sean O'Reilly was a heavyset Italian who was raised by an Irish family. He had made a fortune with a fleet of floating casinos—gambling ships that picked up passengers in the city and traveled beyond the legal limit, plying the players with food and drink along the way. He owned a helicopter and ate fried calamari religiously, claiming that their high neurological functions fueled his business sense.

Ambruzzo easily secured a job as a blackjack dealer, just in time to take part in O'Reilly's annual Gaelic festival. All of the dealers were required to wear green plastic derbies and memorize certain Gaelic phrases, such as *"Céad mile fáilte,"* and *"Erin go bragh."* Sean toured the tables in a shiny suit with members of the Pequot Indian tribe. He was proposing a shuttle to link Foxwoods directly to the city. Casino attendance would boom. O'Reilly would get players coming home rolling hard to recoup their losses. The lawyers had come to close the deal.

Underneath his plastic derby, Ambruzzo had hidden a pile of cards edged with razors. Sean O'Reilly passed his table and Ambruzzo took out the pack and did a fifty-two-card pickup. The razor-edged spades and clubs flipped through the air and landed in arms, foreheads, necks, and hands. The chief of the Pequots had a queen of diamonds in his cheek; one of the lawyers had a three of hearts in his ear. There was confusion, screaming, people knocking one another down as Ambruzzo slipped under the table.

Sean O'Reilly had caught a jack of clubs in his left eyebrow. As he pulled it out, he felt a sharp blow underneath his chin as the bullet from

Ambruzzo's Beretta broke his jaw, then spun its way into his brain. He toppled and in the commotion went unnoticed. Ambruzzo removed the silencer from his gun, left his derby beneath the table and crawled out.

On deck the waves were pitching against the sides of the boat. Ambruzzo stood in the shadows, pausing for a moment to see if he'd been followed. The moon was full, and as it danced along the water beside him, Ambruzzo remembered being afraid of it. When he was a boy he'd had nightmares that the moon was chasing him. Walking home at night, he'd feel it over his shoulder, sense the speed of it coming for him, and break into a run. Ambruzzo held his breath. No one had followed him. He untied a rubber dinghy, set it in the water, and cut loose.

At Nonna's funeral, Ambruzzo thought about flour, yeast, and warm water. He sat in the front pew between Martin Spordonza and members of his grandmother's bocce team. She had collapsed midthrow, the heavy ball spinning from her fingers and landing inches from the marker in the grass. The Old Testament reading was from the Book of Wisdom: *The souls of the just are in the hand of God.*

Martin took care of everything. A mahogany casket, satin lining. An airtight, reinforced-steel casing for the burial. He kept his hand on Ambruzzo's shoulder and realized, as the Mass progressed, that this gesture of comfort was for himself. He pulled out his handkerchief and wept.

Ambruzzo Spagnetti sat on the hard wooden bench and felt nothing. For days he had been listening to other people cry. At the wake, a long line of mourners had snaked from the casket kneeler through the funeral home, out the back door, past the parking lot, down the sidewalk, and shuffled beyond the rectory, where the church ladies patted shoulders and handed out small cups of coffee. Ambruzzo stood alone at the head of the casket, weathered embraces and words of comfort, and waited for his own grief to come.

He was still waiting. He had kissed Nonna goodbye before the coffin closed, and her cheek was waxy and resistant against his lips. Hours later at the funeral, Ambruzzo could still feel the hardness there and became concerned that it did not upset him. He ran the tips of his fingers back and forth across his mouth. Martin sobbed beside him, hiding his face in his hat, his tears staining the fine silk lining of his Borsalino.

Amy Stackenfrach arrived, pushing her two small children in a pram down the marble aisle. One of the children was asleep. The other sucked her toes. Their mother breezed by the altar and parked them in front of a confessional.

"I'm married," she said later during the reception in the church basement. She tested a bottle on her wrist. "I'm happy too."

Ambruzzo told her he was glad. He watched as

the milk dripped from the rubber nipple, slid across the delicate veins at the base of her hand, and curled around the bone. He asked her husband's name. He asked where he worked. He asked what time he usually got home. Amy answered him, then packed her children into the backseat of her minivan. She handed Ambruzzo a cardboard poster tube and told him she was sorry.

Later that evening Ambruzzo opened the tube. Inside was a charcoal drawing of a buffalo. The animal was grazing, its heavy woolen head bent to the grasses of the prairie.

He began to say his rosary at night.

From Montana, Martin Spordonza wrote Ambruzzo a letter. He was sitting by a river. There were mountains behind him. He felt close to his soul, but missed the antipasto. He asked Ambruzzo to send him some fresh Italian meats, a jar of olives, and a cut of Parmigiano-Reggiano. With the family no longer under his supervision, word was out on Rocco Briolli's hit. Martin warned about retribution. He told Ambruzzo that he was his father.

When he tracked down Amy's husband, Ambruzzo found him thin and troubled looking. How easy it would be, he thought, for this man to be trampled. In the scope of Ambruzzo's rifle, Amy's husband scratched his nose. He took out the keys to his car and unlocked the door. He threw his briefcase into the backseat, climbed in, started the engine, pulled to the edge of the parking lot, paused, turned, and glided into traffic. He was whistling.

That night, Ambruzzo tried again. He climbed the tree by the side of their house. He could see inside the bathroom. Amy's husband was flossing his teeth, staring at himself in the mirror. His mouth opened wide and twisted one way, then the other, as he reached for the molars. In the next room, Amy sat on the edge of their bed in a bathrobe. She stood, walked to the window, and opened it. Ambruzzo was fifteen feet away.

Her face was tired. There were lines around the corners of her mouth that made her look like she was frowning. Her hair was tied loosely in a braid. She put her hands on the sill, then brought them back and crossed them over her chest. She turned toward the bathroom, and as she was about to go in, she looked back into the night where Ambruzzo was hiding, and waved.

At the Sons of Italy, Ambruzzo learned that he was being followed. The Briolli family, along with the cast and crew of *Tosca*, had hired a team to take him out. Ambruzzo received the news calmly. He ordered himself a sandwich. He bit into the hard, crusty bread, and tomato seeds got caught in his teeth. He ran his tongue over the tiny bumps. He made no effort to remove them.

Ambruzzo was still waiting to feel something. Inside there was nothing but a dull vibration through the ice, but in the darkness of Amy Stackenfrach's yard, with the bark of the tree against his back, he had come close. *Hello*. It greeted him, and by the time he realized he wanted to wave back *hello*, she had turned, walked into the bathroom, and slid her arms around the waist of her husband.

Ambruzzo put his guns away. He got rid of his knives, his chains, his hatchets. He donated his power drills to charity, along with his chain saw and portable freezer. He flushed his collection of cyanide and barbiturates. He sent all of his black leather gloves out to the cleaners and never picked them up.

He was in Nonna's bakery. He was thirty-four years old. The cash register rang just like when he was a boy. It was after dark. The moon was out. The shot came through the bakery window.

He had been waiting for it. To pass the time, he had read Nonna's cookbooks. In the margins he discovered notes in her bold cursive, accented with exclamation points: *Lemon, no vanilla! Two pinches baking soda!* <u>*Walnuts! 350°!*</u> $\frac{1}{4}$ *cup milk!* Ambruzzo heard her voice, insistent, shouting these directions. He turned the pages, looking for her hand.

There is always a moment, before a person dies. Ambruzzo spent his thinking of marzipan. He looked up the ingredients: almond paste, egg whites, and confectioner's sugar. When he was a boy, Nonna would roll the paste and slice it into coins. Ambruzzo would mark the candy with stamps—flowers, crosses, and teddy bears—his own personal currency. He would eat them, one after the next, until his taste buds were numb and he could no longer sense the sweetness.

There was flour on the counter. Ambruzzo dipped his fingers in it and rubbed them together. He could feel the hit man watching on the other side of the glass, the careful placement of the gun. He lowered the book, lifted his head, and rounded his shoulders. If the shot was clear, it would come to his heart.

TALK TURKEY

J oey Rudolph's mother was the only waitress at the only diner in town. When exactly she began expecting a child was a subject much debated by the neighbors. There were rumours that the father was an enlisted man killed in the war. Some said he was a traveling salesman. A few people suspected that it was someone from town, a man who already had a family.

Regardless, Joey's mother did not go away to a home for unwed troubled girls, and she did not take a bus into the city with a smudged address clutched in her hand. She remained at home with her widowed mother, and she continued waiting tables until her belly started to grow. She did not go to the hospital. She had her baby in the bed that she had left her childhood in, and when she heard Joey cry, she asked her mother to take him away. The boy was never baptized, but his mother showed herself at every church event and planted him among the other children like a threat.

"How did you end up with him as a partner?" Danny Minton's mother wanted to know.

"I didn't choose him," Danny said. "We were assigned by the teacher."

"And what about Ralph Kurtz?"

"We're all part of the same group. It's only for history." Danny covered his head again with the towel and leaned over the pot of boiling water on the stove. Steam rolled across his face and billowed out from the edges of the terry cloth. Behind him, at the kitchen table, his father snapped the newspaper.

"You'll probably have to do all the work," Mrs. Minton said. She rubbed Danny's shoulder. She thumped the back of his chest. "How's it now?"

"I'm fine."

"No, you're not."

Mr. Minton snapped the paper.

"I know Ralph is your friend, but remember what happened to *his* mother," Mrs. Minton said. "That kind of cuckoo thing runs in the family."

"He gets the best grades in school."

"That's because his father works on the principal's car for free."

Danny inhaled the steam coming off the water. He knew why Ralph did well in school. It was because Ralph's father beat him when he didn't.

Mr. Minton snapped the page again.

His wife walked over to the kitchen table and took the paper away. "Don't you care about our son's future?"

"I already know his future," Mr. Minton said. "He's going to work right here, for me."

When Mr. Minton returned from the war, he had ideas of becoming a poet. But his wife was pregnant and his father was old, and someone had to run the turkey farm. For thirteen years he had fixed fences, hammered together shelters, prepared feed, and cut the fields—sitting behind the tractor with a grimace, the steel blades slicing through the grass like meat. When it was time for the harvest, he packed the birds into crates and hired a truck to take them to the slaughterhouse. A few days later they were plucked and trimmed and in the freezer at the market down the road.

His son, Danny, was allergic to turkeys. This was clear to everyone but Mr. Minton, who was convinced that the boy's constant illness was due to laziness and a lack of grit. Mr. Minton blamed his wife for spoiling their child, for making him weak, for spending too much on high-powered vacuum cleaners. Mrs. Minton replaced the feather pillows with foam, the down comforters with cotton quilts. She stocked up on Vicks and insisted on getting doctors' advice. She placed her hand on Danny's forehead, and all the while Mr. Minton's disappointment in his son was growing, hidden away inside him like a cyst.

By the time Danny arrived at the library, Ralph was already there, a center table in the reference room staked out and covered with books. Ralph Kurtz was a quiet boy with dirty fingernails. He was also

Danny Minton's best friend. He knew when to stand by him (two boys with sticks) and when to step aside (one girl with blanket). His mother was in an asylum in North Hampton. After she gave birth to Ralph, she'd stopped wearing clothes and started hearing voices. Mr. Kurtz signed her over to the state, and raised Ralph alone at the family gas station.

"Where's Joey?" Danny asked.

Ralph turned a page of *The History of Meat Production*. "Periodicals."

Danny looked over at the racks of newspapers on poles, the magazines with plastic covers. Joey was reading the latest *National Geographic*. He liked to collect the maps, and would tear them out of issues if the librarian wasn't looking. When his mother worked the late shift, he'd spread them across the card table in their kitchen and imagine himself going places.

"Look at this," said Ralph. He pushed the book he was reading across the table toward Danny. On the page was a series of photographs of birds being killed in a factory—hung upside down by their feet from a moving chain, dunked into a vat of boiling water. "Why do they do that?"

"The feathers come off easier."

"But they're still alive."

"They've got tiny brains," Danny said. "My dad says they barely feel it."

"Gross," said Joey, coming up behind him. "Is that what it's like inside the slaughterhouse?"

"I've never been," said Danny. His mother wouldn't allow it.

Ralph handed each of them a piece of paper. "I've prepared a list of topics."

"I'll take the dead birds," said Joey.

When the boys were finished with their report, they went to the Mintons' farm for lunch. There Mrs. Minton fed them baloney sandwiches. She asked after Ralph's father, but said nothing to Joey. Danny could tell he was going to get it when the others left.

After eating, the boys went outside and started teasing birds, running along the sides of the fence pretending to have food, the turkeys following back and forth like schools of fish, as if they had been hypnotized.

"They really stink," Joey said.

Danny nodded, although his nose was plugged and he could not smell them. "It's their poop."

"Do they have names?"

"Not really," said Danny. "We only keep them for about twelve weeks."

Joey picked up a stick and began to hit the fence with it. The turkeys watched, bobbing their heads up and down together as if they were silently agreeing to one thought.

"Wait," said Ralph. "Did you hear that?"

Danny sneezed. "I didn't hear anything."

Ralph put his fingers on his temples. He closed his eyes. "I am receiving a message from the turkeys."

Danny smirked. "What'd they say?"

"Please don't boil us."

"Come on."

"They say we should go to Hollywood."

"What for?" Joey poked his stick at a large white tom on the other side of the fence. The bird looked back at him, turning its head to see with one eye and then the other.

"The signal is fading," said Ralph, creasing his forehead, squinting. "Wait, wait, I've got it. They say that's where your father is."

Joey shoved him hard against the fence. Ralph hit the post and went down. After a moment Ralph rose to his knees. His lip was split. The turkeys were gathered behind him, wanting to be fed.

"You're lucky I don't beat up crazy people."

Ralph stood. He brushed himself off. "Sorry."

Joey shrugged. He threw the stick far into the field. A small group of turkeys broke from the crowd and ran after it.

"They say he's a movie star," Ralph said quietly.

Joey turned. "Which one?"

"Robert Mitchum."

"Shut up."

"You do kind of look like him," said Danny.

Joey touched a finger to the dimple on his chin.

"Bullshit," he said. But there was a part of him that wanted to believe. Danny and Ralph could see the weakness even as Joey began to laugh to cover it up.

★   ★   ★

The report was a disaster. Danny had typed up only half of their notes. Joey recited a gruesome description of the killing floor, and Ralph tried to save the day by singing a song from the labor movement. Mrs. Johnson gave them a C minus.

"What are you so worried about?" Joey asked. "We passed."

Ralph bit his fingers.

"It's my fault," said Danny. "Do you want me to come over and tell your dad?"

Ralph shook his head. He had done it on purpose. There was a part of him that always wanted to do the worst thing possible, and when he was finished he would stand back and look, frightened and knowing what was coming to him.

When he put his report card on the table, his father leaned back in his chair and tucked his arms tightly across his chest. Mr. Kurtz had grown up in foster care, where he was beaten daily. His nose had been broken in three places. He rarely spoke, and when he did it was usually to insult someone. If there'd been someplace else to buy gas in town, people would have gone there instead.

When he was forced to put his wife away in a public asylum, Mr. Kurtz became determined that his son would succeed. He didn't want Ralph to be a grease monkey, to learn how to take things apart and put them together again. He wanted his son to go to college and make a lot of money so his wife could be in a private asylum, where the patients weren't chained to the walls. He didn't want Ralph anywhere near him or the garage. The boy was standing in front of him now, and Mr. Kurtz saw the parts of himself—helpless, uncertain—that he wanted to forget. He began to rub his nose. Ralph braced. He knew it was the windup.

Later Ralph slipped out his bedroom window and rode his bicycle to the Mintons' farm. There were faint glimmers of movement in the yard. He smelled hay and the damp scent of lost feathers. He crouched next to the fence.

A small group of birds moved across the yard, snoods waving like pendulums in the breeze. The moonlight reflected the white in their wings. Ralph caught his breath as they approached him. He could see the bubbling of skin on their heads. The surface looked impressionable, like poured red wax. They watched Ralph as if they already knew his thoughts.

"Am I nuts?" he asked.

He could feel the turkeys moving closer.

Mrs. Minton stood in the doorway, forcing a smile. Joey Rudolph was on her porch, and he was looking for her son. She'd guessed why the teacher had put the boys together: a crazy kid, a bastard, the sick son of a turkey farmer. They were all on the outskirts. Whatever happened to Danny, she would feel it was her fault. "He's cleaning out the shelters."

Mr. Minton had caught his son in the kitchen when he was supposed to be in the fields. Now Danny was raking mounds of dung and feathers out of the wooden hutches into piles, a bandanna around his nose and mouth. The turkeys huddled together away from him, warbling impatiently.

"I've been thinking," Joey shouted when he got close enough. "Maybe we could go on a trip or something."

"Where?"

"Well," Joey said from the fence, "just away from here for a start."

Danny thought about the way his father had looked when he walked into the kitchen. *Good for nothing*, Mr. Minton had shouted. *You don't care about anything!* But Danny cared about many things. He was fourteen years old. He cared about what his father thought, he cared about pleasing his mother, he cared about losing his virginity, and he cared about his friends.

There was a shuffling noise in one of the shelters. Danny jumped. He lifted his rake and held it over his shoulder, like a bat. Ralph crawled out of the small entryway on his hands and knees, blinking into the light, his pants smeared with guano and feathers in his hair.

"What happened?" Danny asked.

Ralph shrugged. A dark line had swung its way across his cheek, and his lid was swollen and faintly blue. He touched the eye delicately with his fingertips, as if he were measuring it.

Danny offered his bandanna, then sneezed and took it back. The boys stood silently for a moment, watching the turkeys enjoy the spring weather. The

141

birds gobbled. They strutted. They stretched their soon-to-be drumsticks.

"When do you want to go?" Ralph asked.

The boys left before dawn. The roads were empty and the pavement was wet with dew. Danny could feel the money he'd stolen from his mother's purse in his pocket. When he got close to the gas station, he saw Ralph standing out front with a flashlight, a yellow slicker with the hood pulled up and a pair of goggles strapped to his forehead.

Together the boys rolled Mr. Kurtz's old Chevy into the street. Ralph held on to the steering wheel through the driver's window, and Danny pushed from behind. They continued like this until they reached the crossroads, where they pulled the car onto the grass and waited. They kept their eyes on the field, and before long they saw Joey coming through it. He was carrying a blanket and a lunch box.

For days they lived on peanut butter sandwiches. They braked at truck stops to piss and drink coffee. Along the way, Joey taught Danny and Ralph how to drive, swerving along back roads, stalling at inter-sections, grinding the gears. They found a Salvation Army and took showers. They ate bag after bag of marshmallows. They told one another jokes, stories, tricks they'd learned as kids, and things about their lives they never knew or thought they'd say to anybody, just from the sheer boredom of the hours.

★   ★   ★

The tire went near Amarillo. It was a beautiful explosion. The Chevy shimmied across the road as if a ghost had suddenly taken hold of it. Joey hit the brakes and the car bucked, then ground to a halt, the remaining rubber flapping against the pavement. Outside, the earth was a deep red color, touched with bits of scraggly shrubs scattered across the infinite space like a flock of desolate birds. The windows were covered with dust and the road went straight on to the horizon.

The boys sat on the hood of the car and listened to the engine ticking. It was almost dinnertime. They split a peanut butter sandwich and a cigarette three ways and waited patiently for help like children. They did not doubt that it would come. An hour later, when they saw the flash of the setting sun hit the windshield of a faraway truck, Joey pulled off his T-shirt, swung it over his head, and hooted.

They changed drivers when they hit new places. Joey got Elk City, Santa Rosa, and Kingman. Ralph got Shamrock, Albuquerque, and Needles. Danny got Tulsa, Gallup, and Barstow, all the way up to the Lay-Z Motel (no vacancy) just beyond San Bernardino.

They crashed into the motel sign at half past three in the morning. Ralph was stretched in the backseat and he woke up when he hit the floor, the wind knocked out of him and glass tickling his skin. He could see Danny's feet. Somewhere there was the sound of choking. Later he learned that Joey had been sleeping on the passenger side with his head out the window. The impact threw him forward and he landed with his neck against the frame.

In the days that followed, a large black stain would spread across Joey Rudolph's throat as if he had been strangled and released unwillingly. He would not be able to swallow. His voice would come out in a broken whisper as he spelled his name letter by letter for the police. The man writing it down would have to bend over and listen closely so that he could hear.

None of the boys had a license. They were put in a temporary hold at the station. There Ralph chewed his fingers, Danny kicked the wall, and Joey leaned back on the cot and watched the ceiling. It was covered with spots, and he wondered if they were oil or water. Then he turned his face away from the other boys so they would not see him cry.

"I guess I fell asleep," Danny said.

"You guess?" Ralph tore off a piece of skin. "What's going to happen?" He meant when the fathers came.

Danny walked over and pulled at the door. It was locked. "They're going to kill us."

Mr. Kurtz got a call from the state police. The Lay-Z Motel sign had been destroyed and the owner was pressing charges. The boys were all minors and had to be released to a guardian. The arraignment was in two days. Someone was going to have to fly across the country and pick them up.

Mrs. Minton suggested that only one of the fathers go, but the men wouldn't hear of it. They didn't want someone else cleaning their mess. Together they went down to the diner to tell Joey's mother where her son was. They'd lived through the Depression. They'd been in the war. In trouble you take care of your own.

On the plane to California, Mr. Kurtz sat very still and thought of different ways to break his son's arm. It was the first time he had ever been in an airplane and he did not enjoy himself. He counted out the miles as they traveled and tried to calculate how much each one was costing him. All of the money he had saved for Ralph to go to college was being spent on the plane tickets—one over, two back. The only way his son could attend a university now would be if he won a scholarship on his grades. He would have to be able to write. This is why Mr. Kurtz planned on only breaking Ralph's left arm.

Mr. Minton sat beside him and wrote on the back of a paper bag designated for motion sickness. This wasn't poetry. It was a list of everything he was going to make Danny work on when they got home, starting with the old outhouse and continuing piece by piece through the property; all the hardest, roughest jobs that he'd kept for himself. Mr. Minton peered through the tiny window of the airplane. The clouds rolled out in every direction. He thought about Robert Frost and "The Road Not Taken" and thought, *Sometimes you don't get a choice.*

Without looking at their sons, the fathers filled out the paperwork for all three boys at the police station, met with the appointed lawyers, and negotiated a sum with the owner of the Lay-Z Motel, which they split between them. Then they went to a local diner and bought everyone some food. The boys were hungry. They ordered sandwiches and Cokes. The fathers ordered chili and scraped their bowls angrily with their spoons. Everything that was wrong with their lives was on account of these dishes.

When they were finished, Mr. Minton handed Joey an envelope.

"It's from your mother," he said.

The boy opened it. Inside was a letter and forty dollars. Joey read the letter. Then he put it down and looked at the fathers. Mr. Minton cleared his throat. Mr. Kurtz signaled the waitress for the check. They paid for the meal. Afterward, each of the men gave Joey another twenty dollars. Then they shook his hand and wished him luck.

Ralph and Danny never found out what the letter said. They wondered if it had instructions to go to a nearby relative, or if it enclosed Joey's father's address, or if it simply told him goodbye. What happened next happened fast—Ralph and Danny were leaving and Joey was not. They didn't know if it was a joke or a test. Their fathers held on to their shoulders as they passed through the glass doors of the diner. When they glanced back they saw Joey with his purple throat, surrounded by empty plates, fastened in the deserted booth as if he'd already become a memory.

On the plane, as the miles began to stretch the distance, Ralph and Danny sat awkwardly with their seat belts fastened. This was a different kind of excitement. Their ears popped, their stomachs lurched, and their fingers gripped the handles of the seats as the wings dipped. When they were feeling brave, they looked out the window. When they weren't, they bit their lips and thought of home.

They returned to school three weeks after they had left. Ralph was somber and had his arm in a sling. Danny had tiny stitches on his face where the glass from the windshield had gone in. Together they greeted their fellow students with awkward relief.

Later that week the janitor removed Joey's desk from the classroom. The man opened the lid and hunted through what was there: a dark red notebook, textbooks for English and history, an empty pack of cigarettes, a stack of graph paper, a small black comb, a few broken pencils, and what had once been a sandwich wrapped in wax paper—a purple and blue and green monster of spores and rot that had been festering and transforming and continuing to thrive all the while beside them in the dark.

★　　★　　★

When the cast came off, Ralph's arm looked pale and withered. It no longer matched his right. He came to school the following day with a postcard from Flagstaff, Arizona, that read: *Seems longer coming back!*

"It's been months!" Danny said. "Is he walking?" They pulled down the map of the United States in front of the blackboard. Danny marked Flagstaff with a piece of tape. The card made its way around the room, sparking conversations and stirring the other students from their seats. They argued over where Joey had been and what he had been doing, but mostly they thought—*He's alive*—and wondered how long it would take for him to come home.

Danny thought they should bring it by the diner to show Joey's mother. He was trying to be responsible. Mr. Minton had taped the bag for motion sickness to the refrigerator, and Joey was making his way through the list, breaking down the old outhouse, shoveling through a century of waste. With his mother's help, he bought a respirator from a catalog and wore it all day long at the farm. He gritted his teeth through sneezes and thought about Joey and walked around feeling numb. He touched his throat. He couldn't shake how their friend had looked when they left him.

Ralph was reluctant to give over the postcard. He didn't want to go. He said Joey's mother wouldn't care. "She's the one who left him."

Danny went to the diner by himself in the afternoon, when he knew it wouldn't be too busy. He sat at the counter and ordered a milk shake. Joey's mother was standing at the entrance of the kitchen and smoking a cigarette. She looked like a cake under glass, beautiful but tasteless.

"Excuse me," said Danny, even though he knew. "Are you Joey Rudolph's mother?"

She put down her cigarette and held still for a moment before exhaling. She was wearing makeup. Danny could see where she had missed a spot on the side of her face—a blotch of lighter skin, like the peel after a burn.

"That's me," she said.

Danny handed her the postcard. The afternoon sun was blinding against the metal edge of the jukebox, the chrome of the napkin dispensers. He suddenly felt he shouldn't have come. Joey's mother looked at what he had given her and smiled hard.

"This isn't his handwriting," she said. "It isn't even post-marked. Are you trying to be funny?"

Danny didn't know what to say. He held on to the glass his milk shake was in. His fingers were cold and wet, and he felt like a fool, because he knew then that Ralph had done it. Joey's mother snapped the card down in front of him and turned away to sweep her tips off the tables.

When he got home Ralph was waiting for him. Danny handed the card over and sat on the fence. They were still friends, and they would still be friends when Ralph left for college and when Danny got Samantha Rimes pregnant. They'd see each other when their fathers had strokes and Mrs. Minton dyed her hair and remarried. They'd sell the farm and the garage and move away and wonder how the other was and then they wouldn't.

The turkeys hurried across the field. They pecked at one another when they got too close. Ralph tore the postcard from Flagstaff into pieces and fed it to them.

"It's not real food," he said, but they didn't care. They just wanted to get something inside while they could. October had started and the cold nights had come and it wouldn't be long before they were on the table.

HOW TO REVITALIZE THE SNAKE IN YOUR LIFE

He is inherited. A Colombian red-tailed boa constrictor left behind by a man named Fred, who wears black eyeliner and is briefly her lover. She meets Fred on the street. He picks up a pair of underwear that has dropped from her laundry bag into the gutter. The panties are stained and falling apart—she should have thrown them out long ago—but now here they are, in a stranger's hands.

"They're clean," she says. It is all she can think of. Before she finishes, he has lifted them to his nose.

He seems harmless—Coffee?—and has blue eyes. They walk past a café and she invites him upstairs. It has been years since a man was inside her apartment. She feels proud of herself, a little giddy, and a little scared that she has let him in. He offers to fold, and together they spread her sheets across the room, match corners, and double them into tiny packages, each crease moving them closer.

"What's this?" He points to a large black book with a skull on the cover.

"It's for my anatomy class," she says. "I used to be in medical school."

"Creepy." He has opened to a page on facial dissection. There is a photograph of a cadaver. The man is placid, eyelids closed, hair shaved, his lips just slightly blue. On the next page the skin is gone, the muscles pulled apart with metal instruments and identified, the mass of white eye hovering unprotected in its socket.

"Why'd you quit?"

"It wasn't for me," she says. This is her standard line. She doesn't talk about the lack of sleep, the isolation, the loneliness. She doesn't say it was because of Mr. Green.

There was a tradition among the anatomy students to give the cadavers nicknames. Her lab partner suggested Mr. Green. Their assigned body was a young man, forty at most, but somehow in the preservation process his skin had turned. It was gray, with an olive hue. Otherworldly.

"Swamp Thing," her lab partner had said.

Their first job was to take out the brain. They would need it saved for next semester, when the class moved on to the nervous system. A small rotary bone saw was used to cut through the top of Mr. Green's skull. She reached into the cavity, and the brain filled her hands. A section was darkened and compressed, and as she pulled the matter out, there was a trail of blood. Even through the rubber gloves she could feel the texture, the weight steeped in experience. She thought of Mr. Green

154

driving a car, brushing his teeth, eating a salad, putting on his socks. She thought of him reading books, trying to remember someone's name, shouting out the answers to *Jeopardy!* She placed his brain on the tray and it held its shape, like a Jell-O mold. Then she turned and quietly fainted.

Fred closes the book. He slides his hand underneath her shirt. "Is this okay?"

She likes that, his asking.

The snake arrives in a pillowcase. Fred releases it in her bathtub. She watches the animal maneuver itself up and down the length of the porcelain. Brown stripes cross its back, brightening to red at the tail. Inside each marking there are two white ovals perched on either side of its spine. Fred's landlord won't let him keep the boa in his apartment. Would she mind? She wouldn't.

They set up the terrarium on her bookshelf. Heat lamps, thermometers, a tree branch for climbing, and a small bucket turned upside down for a hiding place. He warns her to always keep the cage door locked. On the kitchen table, in a small carryout container, there is a mouse, scratching against the cardboard with its nails. Later, she watches the rodent being eaten, still alive but limp, as if it knows its fate and is resigned to it.

Fred paints her nails black. He traces her lips with eyeliner, leaving a dark, severe border that makes her face look like a puppet's. He brings bagels in the morning and stays all day, stretched across her bed in the sunlight. His steel-toed boots are on the floor, his belt unbuckled and his face in her pillows. Across his back are tiny moles and she licks them, sliding her mouth from one to the other, making a trail.

Fred is a conceptual artist. He is vague on details. It is something about being an outsider, belonging nowhere. There are tiny hairs circling his nipples.

"I'm a secretary," she says.

"I don't believe it."

She takes out her silk blouses, her navy skirt suits, her sensible shoes, her pearls. She suddenly wants to show him everything. He picks an outfit, and she tries it on for him, the control-top panty hose cutting into her waist.

"You look like an idiot."

She has been so alone.

At night he goes back to his apartment, and she stands naked in front of the terrarium, watching the snake digest. She reaches her hand inside, touches the swelling, and is almost certain that she feels the mouse breathe. The snake watches lazily, slipping its tongue in and out, and she knows that it is tasting the air for her.

Fred takes her to a concert. There are crowds of men and women outside the building, all wearing black eyeliner on their lips. Their shoes lift them several feet into the air—platforms of dark foam rubber.

The bar is a corridor filled with smoke. There are colored lights at the end for the stage and a small bulb near the cash register for the bartender to count the money. They get drinks and slide into a booth in the corner, his jeans pressed against her knee. The band tunes their instruments and begins to scream. Her ears close out, as if she were going underwater. And this is when Fred leaves her. He gets up to get another drink and never comes back.

As the band finishes their set, she feels a sudden and suspended sense of loss, that strange, floating moment of clarity before falling down a flight of stairs. Fred has left a package of cigarettes in the booth. There is one remaining inside and she dissects it, cutting the paper down the middle, removing the filter, sprinkling the tobacco across the carved-up table, and then lifting her fingers, wanting to eat the scent.

That night she unlocks the terrarium. It is a dare, really. A way of showing that she is not afraid. The snake is in its hiding place. She waits for a moment, to see if it will sense its freedom and come out. When it doesn't she places the phone next to her bed, turns off the lights, and goes to sleep.

She dreams of Mr. Green. He is standing naked at the foot of her bed, the top of his skull open and empty. Her lab partner has been hard at work. The skin on the arms and legs is peeled away. The tendons revealed. The musculature tagged and labeled. Mr. Green reaches for her and she starts, aware of something in the covers. She finds the snake curled at her feet, his tail wrapped around her ankle, a comforting tightness. The sliding, moving pressure across her Achilles tendon spreads up her leg and makes her feel heavy, weighted, as she leans against the pillows.

She decides to leave the cage unlocked. For this, the snake rewards her. Mr. Green disappears from her nightmares, and the roaches that used to scurry around her kitchen are gone. When she opens her cabinet and finds him mingling with the stems of her wineglasses, she knows that he will not break any, and indeed he doesn't. He slides out silently onto her shoulder. She holds her breath as he passes her face—the scales are so close—the flat white underside of his body touches her collarbone. The weight of him there feels like a blessing, and when he winds his way around her arm and then hesitates, squeezing, not knowing where to go next, she walks over to the sofa, to the seat cushions he likes to sleep underneath, and gently lets him go.

At work, she files. She types letters. She prepares coffee and arranges napkins and creamers. Around her people talk about plans for the weekend, or sports teams, or television shows. When they see her pass by, they ask about paper clips. She is in charge of ordering office supplies, keeping a record of sticky notes and Wite-Out. The memorization skills she was so grateful for in medical school are now used to recite available sizes and colors.

When the Xerox machine breaks, a group gathers near her desk, pleading. She is the only one who knows the right buttons to push, the nooks and crannies where problems tend to stick. She finds the trouble, near the feeder, a piece of paper folded tightly like an accordion. Her coworkers clink coffee mugs and slap her on the back.

These are her rewards, the highlights of her day. The job is easy. Her coworkers are all good people and she likes them. Her boss is kind and apologizes before assigning work. *I'm so sorry.* As if collating were the hardest possible labor.

"Don't worry," she says. "It's not a problem."

At five o'clock she trips getting into the elevator. People move aside, but no one helps her up, as if they know she is here on false pretenses. The door closes and the car goes down. She sits for a moment on the floor, feeling the pull, and thinks about the snake sliding around her things at home.

The smell of Fred has left her sheets. She almost does not notice when it happens, and then she does. She has not washed the sheets for this very reason, rolling in dirt and pieces of her own skin for over a month. She feels abandoned by the smell, like a patient deserted in the middle of an operation, chest open, ribs spread.

She goes back to the club, sits in the same booth,

drinks the same weak vodka tonic. The band is different, bearded. They harmonize. One of them softly plays the bongos. The crowd is wearing browns and oranges, ponchos and sandals. She puts her feet up so no one will sit next to her.

Mr. Green had a family. A wife and two daughters. When she was still in school, she looked up his file, using the hospital database. Two years before his death he'd broken his leg while trimming the branches of an apple tree. He fell from the ladder, dragged his body to the car, and drove himself to the hospital. The doctor who set the bone had written in his notes: *Strong tolerance for pain*. But what had killed Mr. Green was an aneurysm, a blood clot to the very brain she'd been holding in her hands. A better student would have been able to tell just by looking at it.

The snake finds somewhere else to feed. This is the first sign of trouble. She comes home late from work—two heavy brown paper bags in her hands—one full of Indian takeout, the other containing two white mice left over, the pet store owner has told her, from a high school experiment. They are slightly stunned from running mazes. She calls out to him sweetly, flipping on lights, walking through rooms, and finds him curled up on the sofa, fast asleep, a suspicious lump in his midsection.

She draws up a list of his favorite things—silk pajamas, hamsters, the small indentation around the drain of the bathtub—then does her best to provide them. Wears silk pajamas for days until they stink; adjusts her faucets so that a continuous stream of lukewarm water maintains the level of moisture in the hollow of the drain; keeps an extra hamster in a cage underneath the sink; concentrates on the positive.

When this doesn't work, she plays hard-to-get. Ignores him for days and then gets angry when he doesn't notice. She decides he needs punishment. She locks him in the cage without food for two weeks. Then one day she pretends she has just discovered him there. She says, *Who did this to you?* And *Poor baby!* Then she springs the hamster on him. He takes hold of the animal, unhooks his jaw, and begins to swallow. She thinks about what it must be like to take yourself apart and fit anything inside of you, no matter what size, and still be able to put yourself back together when it's over. She waits until he gets the lump halfway down, then sings him a Marvin Gaye song. At night, she slips into bed quietly and waits for him to come to her. She checks to see if he is back on her ankle. She tries hamster number two.

He seems bored. He spends a great deal of time curled up in the water of her toilet bowl. She hates it when he does this. His body leaves long, thin trails of wetness across the apartment. She begins to wonder why she doesn't have cats, like any other, normal single woman.

*   *   *

Mr. Green is back. She has not seen him for months, not since she let the snake out of his cage, but there he is one night, stepping out of her bathroom, the sports section of the newspaper in his dissected hands. She can see the progress that her class has made. They must be up to chapter seven. The chest has been removed, the ribs, clavicle, and sternum cut. The liver is exposed. The lungs fold gently over his heart like hands.

He grins at her, though his lips are gone, and she knows he is saying she has lost her charm. Soon there will be nothing left of him, and she feels the same peeling away inside, a hollowing out, a gradual emptiness. The kitchen clock is humming loudly. He opens the refrigerator and steps in.

She is thankful for her job. Thankful for the coffee, the good-mornings from her cubicle neighbors, the hum of her computer as the switch turns on. Thankful as well no one seems to notice that she is not doing any work. She is simply moving papers around on her desk, arranging them into folders and then taking them out again, stapling them together and then prying the staples out, standing by the Xerox machine and copying the same page, over and over.

The page is a spreadsheet. In small connected boxes it depicts the company hierarchy as if it were a family tree. With a glance over the chart, it is possible to know instantly who people are, where they belong, and what their relative power is. All of her coworkers have been mapped out, like stepping-stones. In the lower right-hand corner, underneath her boss, there is a thin line with her name attached.

Every few months this spreadsheet is revised to reflect promotions, demotions, new hires, and pink slips. It is a game board, and she has remained in the same spot. She has been too passive, she realizes. She has never worked to make more of herself than she is. It was the same in medical school. She remembers the sense of failure after removing Mr. Green's brain. How it took hold of her with a wave of nausea and pulled her into darkness. When she woke up, the rubber gloves were still on her hands. They were wet and smelled of formaldehyde—the skin showing through. She took them off and her fingertips were wrinkled.

What she needs is chicken soup. Something healthy, to bring her strength back. As she is chopping carrots, she sees the snake, curled into the mixing bowl. She reaches out to stroke him and he raises his head, looks her steadily in the eye, and gives out a long, low hiss. She freezes. When he returns to his coils, she thinks about how easily the knife in her hand could slide through him—a cut into muscle, the slit of blood, and the hard ca-chunk as the bone snaps. She could slice him up like zucchini, like a baguette. She has never dissected a snake before, but she has done cats and dogs and fetal pigs and worms. She can do this.

She is ready when he leaves the toilet. He stretches out on the radiator and she picks up the butcher knife. In one clanging blow, she detaches his tiny head and sends it rolling underneath the couch. There is less blood than she expected. For a minute or two, his body writhes and twists. It falls to the floor and she jumps on a chair and waits. She waits some more, then steps down and pokes the body with her knife. She gets the broom from the closet and sweeps the head into a dustpan. Among the hairballs and spare change, it looks like something she might get in a plastic bubble from a dime machine on the way out of the supermarket. She goes to the bathroom and plops the head in the toilet. It sinks to the bottom. She flushes.

After that it is easy. She takes out her old dissection kit—scalpel, forceps, needles, probes, and scissors. She makes a clean incision along the length of his body. Identifies his trachea, esophagus, heart, and lungs; liver, stomach, gallbladder, intestines, and kidneys, as if she were still in school. She tosses the guts in the garbage, peels back the skin. What's left is a yellowish meat.

The buzzer rings. It is Fred.

"Come on up," she says. The skin goes into the garbage, the dissection kit stored away, lipstick smeared on before he knocks.

"I'm sorry about the other night." Fred scratches his cheek in the doorway. His eyeliner is smudged. "I ran into an old friend."

164

"That was three months ago."

Fred shrugs. He looks around the apartment. He sees the terrarium. "You let him out."

"Yes."

"That's not a good idea."

Now it is her turn to shrug. She waits for him to kiss her.

"I got a new apartment," Fred says.

The refrigerator door opens. Mr. Green climbs out. There are three pieces missing from his heart: the wall of the right atrium, a portion of the left ventricle, and above that, the pulmonary valve. His lungs have been removed and she can see his bronchial tree, spreading out like roots on either side of the aorta; a set of skeletal wings, bare branches. She glances over at Fred, who is speaking to her.

"I've come to take my snake home."

"He likes to hide," she says. "You'll have to wait until he comes out. I'm cooking. Would you like some?" And Fred says yes.

She decides to fry. On the chopping block the snake meat is soon in pieces. She dips them in buttermilk, rolls them in flour, throws them in a pan while Fred looks around the apartment, takes the seat cushions off the couch, pokes at a pile of dirty clothes on the floor. Mr. Green watches all of this, amused.

"Dinner's ready."

Fred sits at the small table in her kitchen. He is uncomfortable. She can tell. But he does not seem to notice that Mr. Green is sitting across from him, scratching the hole where his ear used to be with the bone of his finger. Is there lipstick on her teeth? She runs her tongue over them. She hands Fred a plate.

The fried snake is greasy. She has arranged it on lettuce. Mr. Green leans over and steals a bit of meat. He has no stomach; the food travels right through him and lands on the floor. When the lab partner takes his heart, he will be nothing but bones. Still he continues to snatch the pieces away, until a small store builds beneath his chair.

Fred spears the snake with his fork. He turns it over and inspects it before tasting. She stands next to him with her apron on, waiting for him to swallow. He takes his time. He chews. She can see his throat constrict. The piece goes down and Fred looks at her, surprised. He says, "This is good."

GALLUS, GALLUS

A lan Perkin was a short, balding man who was very good at getting other people to do things for him. He had, for example, never learned to tie his shoes. As a boy, his mother had crouched each morning by his feet as he ate his breakfast, threaded the eyelets on his leather uppers, and pulled the laces together in a bow. When Alan Perkin married, his wife took on this responsibility and dutifully performed it every morning after breakfast. If, by chance, one of his shoes became untied during the day, Alan Perkin would politely ask someone standing close by to do it for him. By the time he had reached the age of thirty, nearly everyone in town had tied Alan Perkin's shoes at one time or another.

Alan Perkin owned Perkin's Candy, famous for its saltwater taffy. He was introduced to the business by his father, who taught him to hire pretty girls just out of high school to stand in the store window and pull. The girls had to be skilled, and would go through a rigorous training program in the back room of the store before being allowed up front. People often made special trips to go to

Perkin's, just to stand outside the large glass windows and watch the pretty girls in their hairnets stretch, attach, and twist the long, shining goo between them. The business was a successful one, in that it allowed Mr. Perkin to provide his wife with an ample house, several servants, and the means to support her hobby of raising chickens.

It pleased Mrs. Perkin to have a morning ritual, and something about the clucking and spreading of chicken feed made her feel productive. Each morning, Mary, the cook, helped Mrs. Perkin on with her apron—a pinafore of sorts to protect the front of her dress from soiling. Then Mrs. Perkin opened the door to the backyard, picked up the basket of seed set there earlier by the gardener, opened her mouth, and began to cluck.

Before her marriage, Mrs. Alan Perkin had trained briefly for a position as a veterinary nurse. One day Mrs. Perkin (née Diana Walmut) turned a page in her zoological textbook and came upon a skeletal diagram of *Gallus gallus*, the wild red jungle chicken of Southeast Asia. She was taken with the curve of the beak, the diminutive skull, and the fine, thin bones that fanned out to form the base of the wings. *It looks like a little freak baby,* she thought. *A tiny freak baby with enormous hands.* Diana, the soon-to-be Mrs. Perkin, wept, and from that moment fell in love with poultry.

Mrs. Perkin slid her hand into the basket of seed. How cool and dry it felt! She ran her fingers back and forth and thought of pebbles, of sand, of starlight. A rustling began in the corner shed as the hens made their way down the ramp. Their tiny heads turned and bobbed together in short, rapid movements, as if it took all the power of their little brains to decide that yes, there was noise, and yes, that noise meant food, and yes, they must move to the noise to get the food.

Mrs. Perkin clucked louder and looked for Romeo, her rooster. Romeo had once been a champion cock fighter. His spurs were cut for steel gaffs, used to rip open the throats of his opponents. His feathers were a glistening blue-black color and his comb was a brilliant yellow. Set against that shining dark plumage, it made him look like a king.

Mrs. Perkin had rescued Romeo from an unruly group of local young men who were backing him in fights across the county. On her way home from delivering Mr. Perkin his lunch one day, she had witnessed Romeo spar with Tootsie, the local favorite. Dust and blood and feathers filled the air. Mrs. Perkin watched and felt a sense of exhilaration. When Romeo ruffled his feathers in triumph, she knew that she must have him. It had taken almost six months for her to bring the rooster back to some form of domesticity, and she guarded that control and presence in his life with a possession close to motherhood.

The basket of seed was now empty. Romeo had missed his breakfast. Mrs. Perkin tapped her foot— one, two. Then she asked the gardener to look for him and went inside to phone the neighbors.

Mrs. Kowalski had not seen Romeo. Neither had Mrs. Bronston. Mrs. Dewipple had not laid eyes on him either, although she had noticed that some of her own chickens were behaving strangely. Mrs. Perkin thanked the neighboring wives, hung up the phone, took her place at the breakfast table, and began to worry.

At that moment Mr. Alan Perkin came downstairs with his shoes untied. He took his seat, spread his napkin across his lap, picked up a small silver spoon from the table, and used it to tap the soft-boiled egg in the tiny porcelain cup in the center of his plate. Everything in his morning routine followed a precise schedule that he left, each night before, with the butler.

"Good morning, my dear," said Mr. Alan Perkin. His wife did not answer him. She was looking out the window and wondering where Romeo could be. This bothered Mr. Perkin. When he came to his breakfast table, he announced his arrival by greeting his spouse and expected a cordial reply.

"*Hello*," he said. His wife had upset the balance of his day and he wanted her to know it.

Mrs. Perkin did notice the change in tone of her husband's voice and it immediately aggravated her. Her jaw tightened and she turned her chair slightly, away from the table.

This move worried her husband. He mentally flipped through his behavior over the past week (an anniversary? her birthday?) and came up empty. He ate his soft-boiled egg in a confused silence. His wife ate nothing and continued to look out the window. Soon it came time for Mr. Alan Perkin to leave for work. He checked his watch, put down his spoon, and waited for his wife to tie his shoes.

Mrs. Perkin gazed at the yard outside. She remembered running her fingers along Romeo's neck, and how he would bob his head when she touched him, as though he were enthusiastically agreeing with something she'd said.

Mr. Perkin cleared his throat. He was very good at getting strangers to tie his shoes, but he was not used to using his persuasive charms on his wife.

"It's nine-thirty," he said. "I need to go to work."

"Then go," Mrs. Perkin said.

"I can't very well go without my shoes!"

Mrs. Perkin jumped in her chair. She was not used to being shouted at, especially first thing in the morning, and most certainly not at breakfast.

"I'm sorry, dear," she said. "I had forgotten." She stood and quickly crossed the floor to his side. She kneeled by her husband's feet. She picked up the laces and drew them as tightly as she could before tying them together in an impossible knot. Then she rose from the floor and left the room.

Mr. Perkin finished his coffee and stood up. He noticed that his shoes were quite snug, and as he exited his house and began his morning jaunt to work, he realized that they were snug to the point of discomfort, and by the time he reached the candy store, his feet were pounding and he was carrying on with a slight limp. He curtly asked one of the cashiers to loosen the knots, but his wife had tied them so tightly that they would not come undone. The cashier suggested cutting the laces to free his feet, but Mr. Perkin was not only an extraordinarily persuasive man, he was a frugal one as well, and ruining a perfectly good pair of laces was, to him, a crime.

"Just forget it," he snapped, and began to imagine torturous ways to get even with his wife. He kicked open the door to his office, threw himself in a chair, and propped his feet up on his desk to release the pressure. It was only then that Mr. Perkin noticed the splash of gray and white along the side of his heel. He swiped it with his finger, brought his finger to his nose, and recognized the smell of the henhouse.

The cashier who had failed at untying Mr. Perkin's shoes was named Michael Sheehy. He was a dark man with a slight frame and a lazy eye that slid around in its socket when he spoke. He had been a cashier there for five years. In that time he had often tied Mr. Alan Perkin's shoes. Michael did not particularly enjoy crouching on the ground and relacing his employer's shiny Italian leathers, but he did enjoy the benefits of being the only male employee at Mr. Perkin's candy store.

Michael Sheehy used to wear an eye patch. When he started at Perkin's candy store, he traded in the patch for a story. He told everyone his sight had been damaged in combat—a near death match with a German soldier on the outskirts of Marseilles. He repeated the story often, whenever he felt he was in jeopardy of losing his job or whenever he saw a customer glancing at the roving eye.

In fact, Michael Sheehy had never been to war. He was disqualified for poor sight and flatfeet. Still the young high school girls working at Perkin's candy store found the eye both repulsive and romantic. They became nervous under its gaze and would shiver in excitement and fear when the man placed a warm hand on their shoulders or against the small of their backs.

When Mr. Perkin slammed the door to his office, Michael felt something inside him pick up and turn sour. He looked over at the girls in the window with their hairnets. They were twisting, turning the taffy into a spiral of sugar and smiling sweetly at the crowd gathered to watch them. They were very clean and very pretty.

Michael cast his good eye on Emeline Dougherty, head taffy puller at Perkin's Candy. Her cheeks were flushed, her long brown hair was pulled back in a net, and her arms moved smooth as a machine.

Michael slid open the back door of the counter and picked a piece of peanut butter taffy. He held it in his hand until he could feel the candy begin to soften and lose its shape. Then he peeled off the wax paper, took aim, and threw it across the store at Emeline.

The taffy hit Emeline in the back of her head. She cried out and a shiny loop slipped and drooped from the pull. Emeline and her partner frantically tried to twist and jerk the goo back to the proper stiffness, but it was too late—the taffy was lost—a soft puddle of maple walnut on the floor.

Emeline Dougherty was not a girl who made mistakes. When she was a child, her father had been tragically killed—smothered accidentally on a Sunday promenade by a mound of bluefin tuna. A faulty crane unloading nets from a fishing boat had snapped on the docks and buried him. For this reason Emeline harbored a substantial fear of the unexpected. Her life became a plan that, with the help of her mother, Emeline mapped out at an early age. In her mind, she saw her future in degrees of longitude and latitude, with projections of normal faults, reverse faults, and anticlinal axes. Her position at Perkin's Candy as head taffy puller was an important contour on her topographic existence: three years of salary to be saved for school to become a dental hygienist. As Emeline watched the candy slip from her fingers, she felt a familiar panic of loss.

Emeline ran into Mr. Perkin's office. She didn't knock. In a high, tight voice she reported what happened, then burst into tears and begged him not to fire her. She turned and showed him the evidence—a wad of taffy stuck fast in a mass of hair and net. Mr. Perkin told Emeline to calm herself and offered her a piece of peppermint-flavored taffy—a defensive gesture he used when he wanted someone to stop talking. He suggested, quietly, that Emeline take the rest of the day off to recover from the incident. Then he told her to send Michael to his office and bent over to resume work on the knots his wife had tied that morning.

Mrs. Perkin was looking for Romeo. Impatient with the gardener's progress, she had called on Mary to bring her "the shawl"—a long and heavy crocheted piece Mrs. Perkin's grandmother had brought from Ireland. She wore it like an armor—doubled over her breast and thrown across her shoulder. She marched down the sidewalk into town, stopped passersby, pulled on knockers, and shouted over hedges.

She was just about to cross Main Street when she heard a squawk. A deep, cackling tone that seized her heart with joy. She held her breath and listened for it again. The sound came and Mrs. Perkin ran in its direction. When she stopped she was standing in front of a large wooden monocle. She squinted her eyes and deciphered the words written across it: DEWEY OPTOMETRY.

Mrs. Perkin knew in passing who Thomas Dewey was and had often strolled by the oversize monocle that served as the sign to his business. But before that day she had never given any thought to what an optometry shop was or what Thomas Dewey did there.

She did not know that Thomas Dewey lived in two small rooms behind his shop, or that he enjoyed reading and rereading James Fenimore Cooper's Leatherstocking series while consuming large amounts of cheese. She did not know that Thomas Dewey's father had owned and operated the shop before him, or that Thomas Dewey's grandfather had operated the shop before that. She did not know that Thomas Dewey's grandfather was originally a blacksmith and had inherited the building when his uncle was trampled by the horses of a passing carriage, or that his large black, assuming anvil was now used by Thomas as a bedside table.

The bell on the door jingled as Mrs. Perkin entered. Thomas Dewey was in the back room, deeply ensconced in a copy of *The Deerslayer* and a piece of Gorgonzola. At the sound of the bell, he reluctantly laid down his book, brushed a few crumbs of cheese off his white coat, and opened the door that separated his living quarters.

"May I help you," he said quietly, for in his mind he was still sliding through the woods with Deerslayer and Chingachgook around the edges of the Huron camp, waiting for the right moment to rescue Wah-ta-Wah.

"Have you seen a black rooster?" Mrs. Perkin asked.

As with most people who spend a substantial amount of time alone, Thomas Dewey often spoke aloud to himself in ways that might be thought embarrassing. Mrs. Perkin's question rolled through his mind and into the woods. Deerslayer picked it up, looked it over, and gave him an answer: "The white bear follows his shadow to find his way in a strange forest."

"What?" said Mrs. Perkin. She had a feeling that something lewd had just been proposed. She gathered the shawl tightly around her.

"I'm sorry," Thomas Dewey said, and blushed. "There are no birds here." He looked to his left, then to his right, as though he did not trust his judgment.

Mrs. Perkin followed his gaze over the rows of eye charts, the cases of frames, the boxes of lenses lined up on the counter, and was reminded of her laboratory in veterinary school. She let go of her shawl and noticed other things: tears in the shades above the windows where the light crackled through, soft gray films of dust and streaks like ghosts on the windows.

"I heard him," she said. "Just a few minutes ago."

"What does he sound like?"

"He has a special voice," said Mrs. Perkin.

"Like this?" Thomas Dewey cleared his throat and imitated an early-morning cock-a-doodle-doo.

"That's quite good," she said. "But his tone is higher, with more vibrato in the doodle."

"Hmm." Thomas closed his eyes, inhaled deeply, and let out another rooster call, quite close to Romeo's.

"Amazing!" said Mrs. Perkin.

"It's something of a pastime." Inspired by Cooper, Thomas Dewey had spent the past twelve years of his life memorizing birdcalls of North America. "Would you like to hear another?"

"I should be on my way, if he isn't here."

"I suppose so," said Thomas.

"But perhaps you could call to him from the window?"

"Of course." Thomas walked around the counter and opened the sash. He cupped his hands around his mouth and let out three different calls. "Those last two were females."

"I'm so grateful."

"You might want to stay a bit, and see if he comes." Thomas closed the window.

"I went to school," said Mrs. Perkin. "I was going to be a nurse."

"I'm sure you would have been a good one," said Thomas.

She clarified: "For animals."

"I see," said Thomas.

A collection of magnifying glasses hung on the wall behind him. They made Mrs. Perkin remember an experiment she had done in embryology: fertilized eggs in different stages of incubation, cracked in a petri dish and studied under the scope. She'd seen mitosis, meiosis, and the development of the body—the bulb of a head, the curve of a spine, two dots appearing as eyes. When the students were finished, they dumped all the samples together in

180

a bucket. Mrs. Perkin had held her broken egg, peered into the enormous mass of yellow, and paused. There were tiny bits of red spotting the yolks where the hearts of the birds were still beating. Later, when she told Mr. Perkin about it, he'd smiled and said, "Mmm. Scrambled eggs."

Mrs. Perkin looked over at the cases of frames on the counter. There were dozens of sizes and shapes—square, round, and oval, silver and gold. "Maybe I need glasses," she said.

"Would you like me to examine you?"

"No. I just want the frames." She picked a silver pair with a thin pattern of vines engraved across the bridge and down the length of the arms. Mrs. Perkin put them on and looked in the mirror. She saw a woman older than she was.

In the bathroom, Emeline tried to remove the taffy from her hair. The high school girls gave words of comfort, but Emeline shunned their offers of grease, soap, and tonic water. She could feel anger prickling along her skin, spreading with exasperation. She broke from the crowd, grabbed her coat from the closet, and left without saying good-bye.

When Emeline was a little girl, her father warned her about emotions. Her mother had always been prone to hysterics, which frequently drove her father out of the house to take long walks along the wharf. He often brought Emeline with him. The two would move along in silence, Emeline taking three steps for every one of her father's, doing her best to keep a look of preoccupation on her brow so that he would not feel the need to amuse her.

On their way back home, Emeline's father would inevitably pause and voice some conclusion he'd arrived at during their stroll. Sometimes they were about his wife, sometimes they were about himself, and sometimes they were for Emeline: "Don't be like your mother," he said. "Stay away from *the feelies*."

Emeline considered this as she walked down Main Street with taffy in her hair. She thought of her father's final moments under the mound of bluefin tuna. She imagined the weight, the cold, wet slickness, the slowing beats of tails searching for water. She wondered if he'd been angry under the pile or if he'd had time to feel anything at all.

As she passed Thomas Dewey's shop, Emeline noticed Michael Sheehy sprawled on the sidewalk beneath the large wooden monocle, a bottle of whiskey under his arm and two long black shiny feathers in his hair.

"Hello," said Michael. "I'm fired."

"Well, you deserved it," said Emeline.

"You deserve a kick in the pants."

"You're drunk."

"Yes."

"What are you doing here?"

He pointed at the sign. "I want to get my eye fixed."

Emeline blushed. She thought of the high school girls imitating him, rolling their eyes and groping one another in the bathroom.

"It's not that bad."

"Yes it is," said Michael, "and you don't have to live with it, so don't tell me what to do."

"I'm not telling you anything!"

"I'm sorry. Forgive me." Michael Sheehy began to cry. He reached up and took hold of her skirt.

Emeline stood perfectly still and tried to control her emotions. The cloth pulled against her hip. Michael lifted the edge and wiped his face. A breeze touched her legs. If her father were here, he would disapprove. She was sure of it.

Inside the optometry shop, Thomas Dewey was giving Mrs. Perkin a sampling of his calls. He had never had an audience before. He puckered his lips and did his best imitation of Deerslayer's whip-poor-will song. Then he tried Chingachgook's secret signal for his lover, Wah-ta-Wah— the chatter of a North American squirrel. Mrs. Perkin listened politely as she kept watch out the window. She peered through the glass, and this is what she saw: the girl who pulled the taffy in her husband's shop, the cashier with the lazy eye who rang it up, and stepping out of the bushes, Romeo.

He looked as though he'd been in a fight. His feathers were ruffled, his comb was torn, and one of his wings was dragging behind him. He stepped carefully, gingerly, circling around Emeline and the man crying at her feet.

He hasn't had any breakfast, Mrs. Perkin thought. *He must be cold and hungry.* She watched Romeo's wing brushing the ground and thought back to *Gallus gallus,* trying to determine which bones had been broken. She thought of the metacarpals, the long, thin, delicate fingers, and wondered if she could ever make them straight again.

Romeo leapt into the air and landed on Emeline's shoulder. She tried to shoo him off, but Romeo knew from his fighting days how to hold on. He dug one claw into her collarbone, the other into the side of her neck, and began viciously attacking her taffy.

Emeline screamed.

Michael Sheehy let go of her skirt and got up from the sidewalk. He had always been afraid of birds. He held his whiskey bottle with both hands and tentatively used it to poke the rooster on Emeline's shoulder.

"Off now," he said. "Off." As he pushed at Romeo with the spout, the bottle slipped from his hands and fell crashing to the sidewalk.

Mr. Perkin heard the glass shatter as he turned onto Main Street. His wife had not brought him his lunch that day, and with the help of a cane, he was irritably making the trip home for a sandwich. Mr. Perkin looked up from his shoes and saw his head taffy puller being attacked. He recognized the yellow comb of his wife's favorite chicken.

Mr. Perkin was a businessman. He did not often miss opportunity. He watched for it, and when it came he took it in hand. Mr. Perkin hobbled to Emeline's side. He raised the cane over his shoulder. He swung, landing a blow to Romeo's head, and the bird toppled to the ground. Mr. Perkin then stood over the rooster and beat it to death with his cane.

There were reasons, Mr. Perkin thought, for doing things. He believed in getting what he wanted. He also believed in taffy. It was his base, on which he had built a life that pleased him. *This is it,* he thought as he broke the rooster's neck. This business, this taffy puller, this missing sandwich. This was who he was. There was blood spilling from the mouth of the bird, pooling on the hard, dry ground. Mr. Perkin moved his feet out of the way and noticed that his laces had come undone.

It was inappropriate, he realized, to ask the girl he had just saved or the man he had just fired to tie his shoes. He glanced down Main Street, then at Thomas Dewey's shop. There was a woman standing at the window in a pair of silver frames, a black wrap across her shoulders. Her fingertips were pressed against the glass, five points spread like a mouth in surprise. Alan Perkin stood, laces trailing, and waited. Surely, he thought, he could depend on her to come.

BLOODWORKS

Richard was tired of asking the same question: Why did you do that? He said this to Lucas after his son stopped completing his homework, after he knocked over an old woman for taking too long to get on the bus, after he ran past the dining room table, grabbed the table-cloth, and turned their meal onto the floor. Richard knew that something was wrong with his son. He walked around at night and thought, *There are too many rooms in this house.*

Richard and Marianne sent their ten-year-old to his room; no TV, no dinner, no dessert. They tried talking, they tried spanking, and finally, when he would not listen or stop smacking his sister, they pinned Lucas to the ground until he conceded, until he stopped kicking, biting, scratching, and went limp, the red slowly draining from his face.

"I don't know how much more of this I can take," said Marianne after sitting on the boy's legs for ten minutes. She was a massage therapist. It had been a long day and her hands were tired. When Lucas was a baby, she loved to touch him. She thought of how he had smelled then, a scent so clean and full of hope it made her cry with gratefulness.

"I think he's asleep," Richard said. Lucas's mouth hung open to the side, a small puddle of saliva gathering on the floor. Richard carried him into the living room and laid him out on the sofa. Then he went to the refrigerator and got himself a beer.

Richard settled into his easy chair and looked at his son. How had he ended up with a child like this? He remembered holding the boy in his arms for the first time. He remembered trying to slip his finger into the baby's tiny fist. He took a sip of beer, knocked his tooth against the bottle, and felt a tingling nerve of pain drive into his mouth. *Like this,* he thought, *I've done everything wrong.*

Marianne was in the kitchen, scraping excess food from their dinner into the garbage disposal. So much macaroni and cheese. Why hadn't she made something better, with vegetables and vitamins? In the past she had tried brown rice, tofu, and tahini, but the family refused to eat it. Eventually she had grown tired of arguing and turned to the cookbooks of her mother, recipes that started with a stick of butter.

On her own she still browsed books at health food stores (broccoli is an upper!); spent afternoons at a Hare Krishna café, quizzing the chef on vegan cooking. She considered potions, spells. She remembered sliding her own toenail clippings into a glass of punch and giving it to a boy she liked when she was twelve, convinced it would make him fall in love with her. Now she pulled out *Joy of Cooking* and checked the index for health and nutrition, studying the metric conversions. She hoped that somehow the next recipe would have an answer, the next one would tell her what to do.

When the school counselor called to say that Lucas was having problems behaving in class, Richard and Marianne accepted her reference to a local clinic. Lucas began to receive monthly sessions of psychotherapy from a middle-aged woman named Dr. Snow, who consulted the *Diagnostic and Statistical Manual of Mental Disorders, Fourth Edition,* wrote a diagnosis on his chart: 314.01—Attention-Deficit/Hyperactivity Disorder, and gave the parents a prescription for Ritalin. It made everyone feel better. Something was being done. Dr. Snow said that his outbursts were a phase, and that by the end of puberty, he'd be over it.

Marianne turned the pages of her cookbook and watched her children playing on the stairs. Lucas was using a flashlight to produce a circle of light on the wall. He dropped down a step and began making shadow shapes with his hands—a goose, then a seagull, then a horse, then a dog. Sarah, their eight-year-old, sat next to him and watched. After a while she tried to mimic what he was doing.

She did not like to admit it, but Marianne loved the girl a little less. A first child settles down and crushes you. Her love for Sarah was different—lighter but full of surprises. She always seemed to be stumbling onto her, like the time she heard voices, opened the bathroom door, and found Sarah standing on a stool, the shampoo and mouthwash and hairspray lined up in conversation along the counter, dental floss hanging like streamers from the medicine cabinet, the sink full of water. She'd made a pool, and the toothbrushes were swimming.

Marianne settled on a recipe for broccoli quiche. She could hear the neighbor's cat outside, prowling the yard. At times its voice was so much like a wailing baby that she would start out of bed when she heard the sound. Then, unable to sleep, she would stumble to her children's rooms, just to make sure that no one had called for her.

Sarah waved her hands in front of the flashlight. "I can't do it."

Lucas took hold of her wrist. He pulled her pointer and middle finger straight, and curved her thumb over the rest. "Stick that one out a little," he said, and Marianne saw the rabbit's teeth appear.

"Now, curl that one in tight, but not too much," he said, and Marianne saw a tiny speck of light become the rabbit's eye.

"Move your thumb," he said, and the rabbit sniffed. It wiggled its ears. Marianne was glad, seeing them like this. It was a rare moment of togetherness. They usually played out of sight, in their rooms. She could hear them sometimes, thumping around, and had to stop herself from making sure things weren't brewing into a fight.

Taking care of two children was harder than anything she'd ever done in her life. Once Sarah was born, Marianne was always tired. She felt that her responsibilities would never end, and that she was a failure as a mother, because there were times when she wanted to leave. To fight the urge, she would lay her two-year-old and newborn side by side on the bed and count their toes, back and forth. Twenty of them. Moving. Perfectly fresh and pink.

Lucas was standing now, twisting his arms to form a new creature in the light. Marianne felt her stomach, the soft mound of loose skin. She thought, *I made those fingers.* She wanted to call out, to ask what kind of animal Lucas was making, but before she could the jaws opened and clamped down over the shadow rabbit, Sarah screaming as Lucas dug his nails into her skin.

Richard's collection of silver dollars was gone. He came home from work, opened the desk drawer, and saw the red velvet coin bag stretched out empty, like a deflated party balloon. He knew right away that Lucas had taken them. Over the weekend, Richard had refused to drive his son to a comic book store in the city. They had argued about it for days. The more Lucas shouted and declared that Richard was going to take him, the more Richard refused to budge, even when

Marianne came to him at night and asked him softly to give in.

"Open up!" Richard pounded with his fists outside his son's bedroom. "Lucas! Open the door!" This was Richard's home. He paid the bills. He'd put the wallpaper up in this hallway, paid for the wiring for this light, painted the trim on this door frame. He tried pushing against the door with his shoulder and realized that Lucas must have put up a barricade. Richard got a chair and sat in front of the room for an hour, glaring at the handle, waiting. When the door finally opened, he forced his way in.

"What did you do with my coins?" Richard shoved the bureau back against the wall and began searching the room. It was dark inside; the shades were drawn. He moved a Hot Wheels racetrack, kicked a pile of clothes on the floor, checked underneath plates and bowls crusted with food on the desk. "Where are they?"

"Get out of my room!" Lucas shouted.

Richard suddenly felt as if he were confronting his own father, dead three years now from Alzheimer's. The old man had been convinced at the end that Richard was a spy, the nurses professional torturers.

"Doors don't lock in this house," Richard said.

"I didn't touch your stupid coins."

Richard tried not to lift his hand and threaten him. The coins came from Europe, India, and South America. His father had kept them hidden at the nursing home. Richard found the velvet pouch while cleaning out the room, stuffing garbage bags full of cardigan sweaters and dirty socks. He hadn't known that his father was a collector. When the drawstring opened, the coins had jingled and he'd felt their worth.

"I'm going to count to three."

Lucas swung his leg back and kicked him.

"That's it," said Richard, and he pinned the boy against the wall.

Lucas spit in his face. "I didn't do anything!" But he had. Sarah told. The coins were in the sewer. He'd dropped them, one by one, down the grate in the street.

Dr. Snow wrote down a new diagnosis in the chart: 313.81—Oppositional Defiant Disorder. She changed his prescription from Ritalin to Mellaril. It will pass, she told them. She'd seen it many times before. He was a good kid. She looked at her notes. They didn't have to worry.

But they worried. When Marianne turned off the television during Saturday-morning cartoons, Lucas took a glass of soda from a nearby table and threw it at her head. It glanced off a bookshelf before shattering at her feet, the cola fizzing against the floor like acid. Marianne spent the next forty-five minutes in the car outside, turning the ignition on and off, on and off.

She liked to sit in the car. Marianne sometimes sat there in the driveway not going anywhere for hours. She enjoyed the quiet, the way it felt to be sealed inside of something, the suction of the air as the door slammed shut. Before she got married, she had driven across the country and spent nights curled in a sleeping bag across the backseat. She had lied to her parents that she was traveling with friends. She had felt no danger.

One night she got caught in a dust storm. Tumbleweeds sprang from the darkness and soared past her headlights while the wind threatened to shimmy the car off the road. She pulled behind a deserted gas station at a crossroads and fell sound asleep, the sand spraying the windows like hail. She woke up to silence in the middle of a Navajo Indian reservation and drove through Glen Canyon at sunrise. She wondered now at her faith in flimsy door locks, in stars turning into morning.

Every day there seemed to be another test. Coming home after work, Marianne heard a shuffling and found Sarah in the crawl space underneath the porch, covered in cobwebs and dead leaves. Lucas had locked her inside for telling about the coins. Marianne unhooked the latch.

Sarah crept out and wiped her face off with her sleeve. She smiled. "Is he going to get in trouble?"

Somewhere over the past year Marianne had lost the ability to communicate with her son. She went through boxes of baby clothes in the attic—tiny sailor suits and booties—she searched his dirty laundry, poking through pocket lint, eyeing his shirts and underwear; she scrutinized his report card, his toothbrush, his bike, the remains of his breakfast, and his issues of *Ranger Rick*. She felt guilty for wishing she were somewhere else, for wanting not to be his mother.

Marianne liked to think of how much worse it could be. She made lists in her head while massaging her clients. Lucas was not setting fires, he was not running away from home, he was not beating people with bricks or bats, he was not mugging people or raping people or torturing animals. He was only a little bit crazy.

What a word, she thought. She had said it many times—that, and others. Insane. Freak. Psychopath. Now they fell from her mouth by accident, like frogs. She felt the words slip out and drop to the floor. It would take a moment or two for Marianne to recover from saying them. Meanwhile, her client on the massage table would be rolling over, ready for the other side. Marianne swallowed down the swampy feeling in her throat and covered her palms in oil.

When Richard was a teenager, he saw a dog in the road one night and purposely ran it over. It was a sheepdog, white and fluffy, a gray spot over its left eye. He stopped the car afterward to look. The dog smelled like an old couch. It had a worn leather collar with a new tag around its neck. Richard touched the dead animal's fur and thought about his father. They had been fighting before he left home. He knew somehow that this is what had made him kill the dog. He stood on the side of the road in the dim blue light of morning and remembered the eyes of the animal reflecting back his headlights; the well of anger flowing into his chest, down his arms, through his hands to the wheel, and how the bump, the thud, the roll of the car beneath him, had lifted his spirits and made it all go away.

Richard wondered now if this is what happened to Lucas. If he did these things to find relief. Richard had never found any, and his father had never found any, and his father's father had never found any; this he knew. Before he died in the nursing home, Richard's father had talked about his own father. Gramps beat the family regularly and spent every night out in the barn, eating straw and screaming. They found the body hanging in the rafters after a hard winter, the old man's face purple, bits of alfalfa stuck to his lips. There was something in the family blood. But Richard had found ways to manage. He had held down a job and had children. When his wife put Lucas in his arms for the first time, Richard had cried. He had wanted a son that badly.

Each year the family sent out a photo of the children for the holidays. Marianne had a stack of the pictures in her hope chest—Lucas as a baby in a miniature sleigh, then with a tiny Santa hat, then holding his sister, propped up and grinning against a pile of fake snow. At the studio the photographer arranged Sarah next to a plastic Christmas tree and gave her a present wrapped in gold and silver paper. She shook it and Marianne watched her face drop as she realized it was empty. Lucas was placed behind, a hand on Sarah's shoulder. The matching sweaters Marianne had knit them didn't quite fit. Sarah's sleeves ended just past the elbows, and the snowflakes stretched across Lucas's chest as if someone had held on to them and pulled.

They were beautiful children. Both had Marianne's dark hair and skin but kept Richard's pale blue eyes. Against the fake fireplace Lucas looked taller, and Marianne could almost picture him as a teenager, posing for his high school yearbook, slight acne on his chin and a faraway look. Sarah wrinkled her nose as if she were about to sneeze. She still had the pudgy cheeks of a baby.

Marianne felt Richard take her hand. She pressed her palm into his and held on. Lucas bent over the fireplace, and she saw that he was whispering in Sarah's ear.

"Leave me alone," Sarah said.

"Face the camera now." The photographer huddled underneath the black curtain.

"Stop it," Sarah said. "Mom, he's pinching me."

"Just look at the camera," said Marianne. "We're almost done."

"But it hurts!"

"Smile," Marianne begged. She could feel Richard tightening his grip.

Sarah's chin dimpled as if she were about to start crying, and suddenly Lucas knocked the present out of her hands and sank his teeth into her arm, tearing a hole in her sweater as she struggled to get away. The silver and gold box was crushed, the Christmas tree knocked over and ornaments broken, before their parents were able to separate them.

Richard insisted on still taking the picture. "We've already paid for this," he said. "We'll take it together, all of us." He stood between the children, his arms pinning each of them painfully to his side. "You better smile." The photographer quickly rearranged the lights. He could not wait to be rid of their family. Marianne stood in the corner, partially covered in darkness. She paused for a moment before stepping forward to join them.

On the way home Lucas kicked Sarah in the backseat, stretching out across the vinyl and digging his heels into her side. Richard kept one hand on the wheel and the other behind him, reaching blindly for his son's legs, trying to stop the fight.

"I wish you were dead!" Lucas shouted.

Sarah pressed her hands against her ears and curled up into the corner.

Marianne looked straight ahead and said nothing. It would be over soon, she told herself. Everyone would go to their room and then it would be quiet. They just had to make it home.

She pictured Sarah and Lucas telling stories to each other like they used to, holding secret meetings under the kitchen table, cutting dragons and pterodactyls out of construction paper.

There was a click in the backseat, and Marianne felt a rush of air. Sarah had opened the car door; it swung into the road, the asphalt rushing underneath in a blur. Her seat belt was undone and she had one leg out, ready to jump.

"What are you doing?" Marianne screamed. "Pull over! Pull over!" Richard swung into the breakdown lane, and as soon as they stopped, Sarah was out of the car, running down the street, and Marianne was after her, reaching out with her arms, trying to catch her daughter before she got too far away.

312.30—Impulse-Control Disorder. Dr. Snow marked the chart and switched Lucas to Seroquel. She said, "It should calm things down a bit." She also said, "Look for ways to help each other."

Richard and Marianne found this difficult, because in truth they blamed each other. Marianne felt Richard troubled Lucas more by confronting him, and Richard felt that she made their son worse by giving in. Every night after the children had gone to bed, they argued, both of them feeling that they had somehow been conned.

They slept on the outside corners of their mattress, not touching, the blankets shifting back and forth. In the morning Marianne crushed Lucas's pills into orange juice and Richard read the paper and tried to ignore the howling in the yard.

"One of these days I'm going to kill that cat."

Something smelled bad in the hallway. It reminded Marianne of the summer, when a squirrel had crawled into the wall by the stairs and died. They'd all held their breath going down the steps until it rotted away. Sometimes she still held her breath when she crossed the spot. Sometimes she thought about the skeleton, frozen in the wall.

Marianne started cleaning. She bought extra Pine-Sol and Bon Ami and went to work, scrubbing down the wallpaper, dusting books. The smell dimmed but continued to hover near Lucas's room. Marianne hesitated at the door. She didn't want to go inside. Instead she disinfected the frame, the doorknob, the molding in the corner. She was spreading rug cleaner over the carpet when Lucas emerged. It was the middle of the day, and he still had his pajamas on. Tiny rockets and spaceships blasted across the flannel. The top was too small for him, the bottoms ending far above his ankles.

"What're you doing?"

"I'm trying to get rid of that smell."

"I don't smell anything."

With the door ajar it was stronger. The stench was behind him, coming from the room.

"Do you have any old dishes in there?"

Lucas stood in the doorway, opening and closing his fists.

"I don't care what it is," Marianne said. "Just get rid of it." She was pleading now.

Lucas dipped his toe in the rug cleaner, then spread the white foam back and forth across the carpet. "Okay."

Marianne felt a wash of relief. It was as if he had forgiven her for something. She touched the back of Lucas's head and he stood still for a moment, allowing this. His hair was thick and vaguely unwashed, so that afterward, when he closed the door and she was left alone, she could feel a thin film of grease left on the tips. She held them underneath her nose and they smelled like sheets that have been slept in too long.

Richard was reading in the kitchen when he heard a thump. It was the heavy sound of a body hitting an object, and it made him drop the newspaper and race up the stairs, his wife abandoning her pots and pans and stumbling behind him. They turned into the hallway and saw Lucas standing over Sarah, trying to pry something out of her fingers. When the boy saw Richard, he jumped into his room and slammed the door.

There was a gash across Sarah's forehead. A dark splitting of skin that seemed to pulse for a moment before releasing a rush of blood down the side of her face. In her hands was a clear plastic bag. When she saw her parents, she held the bag up like a prize. Inside was the body of a kitten, emaciated and stiff, the fur orange and white. A brownish liquid seeped from one of the corners.

"I found it in his closet," Sarah said. "It stinks." She let go of the kitten and began to vomit on the carpet.

"Get some towels!" Richard shouted. The cut looked deeper than he'd thought. He pressed his hand against the opening as Sarah coughed onto the floor. When she started to cry, he lifted her in his arms.

Marianne held out a wet washcloth and a blanket. They needed to go to the hospital, and she kept turning her head to look at the kitten. Richard pushed the plastic bag to the side with his foot. He told Marianne to get the keys. He carried Sarah down to the car. Then he came back for Lucas.

Richard beat the door with his fist. He shoved once, twice, leaning his weight. He could feel his son pushing against him on the other side.

"That's it," said Richard. And he kicked the door in.

Before he put in the stitches, the doctor covered Sarah's face with a sheet. Her body looked pale on the hospital bed, the white cloth giving only the smallest details of her nose and chin. It reminded Marianne of crime scene photographs where something is tossed over the victim's head.

The doctor hummed as he sewed Sarah's skin

together. Marianne was sure he thought she was a terrible mother. She dragged a metal folding chair over to the bed and quietly took her daughter's hand. She couldn't remember the last time she'd held it. Was she six, seven? Had they crossed a street? She noticed that her fingernails looked bitten.

"Almost there," said the doctor. A television in the corner showed a picture of a game show. Someone was winning, but there wasn't any sound.

Down the hall Richard filled out medical forms with a nurse. He stopped at the watercooler on his way back to the waiting room. The stream was weak, but it felt good to wet his lips. He called Dr. Snow from the pay phone, keeping an eye on Lucas slumped over a magazine in the corner.

"The drugs aren't working."

"Sometimes this is the case."

"He's getting worse."

Dr. Snow sighed. "Attacking siblings is quite common." She suggested family therapy. She scheduled a meeting for the following day. They should go home and get some rest. "Order Chinese," she said. "Something easy."

When the car pulled into the driveway, Richard saw their neighbor. He could tell something was wrong by the way her skirt was twisted.

"I don't know what to do," she said as Richard rolled down the window. "My cat won't leave your yard."

"Just a minute," said Richard. He stepped from the car and opened the back. Lucas dashed up the porch stairs, pushing Marianne out of the way as he went through the door. Richard turned to the neighbor. "This isn't really the best time."

"It's all right," said Marianne. "I'll take her." She put the house keys in her pocket and eased Sarah out of the car. It was hard for Richard to look. A large white bandage was taped across Sarah's forehead, and he could see a section of baldness where the doctor shaved her hair.

"What happened?" the neighbor asked.

"Nothing." Richard forced himself to grin. "Just an accident."

"She looks hurt!"

"She's okay." Marianne lifted Sarah onto her shoulder.

"I'm *not* okay," said Sarah.

"You just need some rest."

"I want the TV in my room."

"You'll get it." Marianne carried her daughter up the stairs. "Happy now?" Sarah hid her face.

"So," said Richard. "What's the problem?"

The cat was in the backyard, fixed in one spot.

"I'm very sorry about this," said the neighbor. "I can usually coax her home." Her face trembled a bit as she approached the orange tabby. "Come on now, honey." The cat hissed and swiped at the woman's hand, then hurried back to its spot.

"She might have rabies."

"No!" cried the neighbor. "She's just upset! Can't you see how upset she is?"

He didn't have time for this. Richard rubbed the back of his neck. He tried to think of ways to get rid of them both. The neighbor took a seat in the dirt and began softly snapping her fingers. The cat ignored her, made groaning noises, and used its claws to paw at the earth.

The cat's empty belly swayed, nipples dragging on the ground. When he looked closer, Richard saw that its whiskers had been cut. He knew that cutting whiskers was similar to blinding; animals used them to feel where their eyes couldn't reach. Richard glanced up at the house. The shades were closed.

He went over to where the cat was sitting and pushed at the ground with his foot. Richard's shoe sank into the soft soil, and when it touched what had been buried there, he felt his spirits descend with his wingtip, a turning over into sadness. He thought about what was coming. There were worms, he could feel them, and tiny pebbles making their way into his socks.

MISS WALDRON'S RED COLOBUS

Miss Waldron was an American. When she turned twelve years old, she was deposited in a New Hampshire boarding school to be raised by nuns. She watched from the window of her room as her father drove away in his forest green MG, the wheels leaving a trail of dust on the gravel road. Then Miss Waldron turned to the nun who had been cheerily unpacking her things and slapped her across the face.

This was the first picture taken by the private detectives: Miss Waldron with her hand out, a blur of hair and teeth. The sun was shining through the latticework behind her, sending a patterned shadow of bars across the curtains. The detectives were three educated men from Minnesota. They had seen tornadoes and men killed with pitchforks, but they had never seen a girl hit a nun.

Miss Waldron's father had hired the private detectives to keep an eye on his daughter. Each week they sent a telegram detailing her life—what clothes she was wearing, what kind of cereal she ate, what hour she had hitchhiked to the nearest saloon. Sometimes they sent pictures. These messages were met with silence. The men sometimes wondered if the father read them at all.

Miss Waldron spent the next few years running away. Some of these attempts were more successful than others. At fourteen, she disappeared at the zoo, slipping into the foliage of the primate house. The detectives found her two days later, living with a family of lemurs, her uniform bargained for bananas.

At fifteen, she hired a crop duster with her birthday money. The plane touched down in a field behind the school during a class in calisthenics. The girls finished their round of jumping jacks and Miss Waldron broke from the line, her white legs streaking across the grass. The pilot dropped her off near the train station, where she joined a passing carnival. After reporting this, the detectives received their first telegram—*FETCH HER FROM THE CIRCUS AND RETURN HER TO THE NUNS*—and finally caught up with Miss Waldron a few weeks later in Louisiana, where she was performing as a veiled trapeze artist.

The nuns made an example of her. This example involved the scrubbing of toilets, the repetition of the rosary, and silent but carefully directed guilt. It did not stop Miss Waldron from escaping, but they noticed it kept the other girls from getting close to her. Then came the Italian.

Maria arrived at the convent with an enormous mane of dark hair that fell to her waist and a personal maid whose job was to take care of it.

She was the illegitimate daughter of a contessa and her gardener, drank tumblers of amaretto liqueur, and wore high-necked dresses that were specially tailored to hide a stunning red birthmark in the shape of a penis.

On a class trip to Silver Lake the girls were partnered together for a canoe ride. As they set out across the water, Miss Waldron asked the Italian what she did for fun. Maria spun around, nearly upsetting the boat, and said, *Never will I have happiness away from Fredo.*

Fredo, Miss Waldron soon learned, was Maria's stepbrother from the contessa's brief third marriage. He had thick eyebrows and sideburns that went down to his chin. In the three weeks the new siblings had spent together they managed to commit six mortal sins and forty-seven venial. Maria explained their plans to get married and, as her paddle made soft spirals through the water, said, *You must come visit us*, in a quiet, conspiratorial way that reminded Miss Waldron of characters in a novel, inviting each other over to their country estates.

Maria remained at the boarding school for two months, and during that time Miss Waldron did not run away. She enjoyed hearing about the countries Maria had traveled to and what Fredo had done underneath the dining room table. Maria was scheming to get transferred to a boarding school near her stepbrother's in London. *No more New England,* she said with distaste, and was true to her word. Soon after, she was standing in the front hall with her maid and her luggage and her hair braided neatly, waiting for the driver.

A week later Miss Waldron convinced a team of Navy cadets to infiltrate the boarding school and smuggle her out. She returned one month later (escorted by the private detectives) and brought back stories of submarines and speakeasies, coral reefs and coconuts, a Bessie Smith record, a long black cigarette holder, a pair of high heels, and a venereal disease.

Miss Waldron had seen her father only three times since he dropped her off at the boarding school in his sports car—twice for Christmas and once for a Memorial Day picnic. When he heard what she was being treated for, he arrived at the hospital in a storm—overcoat flapping, goggles strapped to his head, leather gloves in hand.

She could hear him coming down the hall toward her room. This was something the private detectives did not photograph—the girl crouched in the corner in her hospital gown, her legs bare, her hands at the back of her neck, her eyes darting from the window to the door as it slammed open.

He called her a filthy animal. Then he crossed the floor. Then he kicked her. Then he left.

Miss Waldron curled around the ache in her stomach and listened to her father's footsteps. She'd had a fever for weeks. The sweat covered her body in a thick paste. It hurt so much to go to the bathroom that she had stopped eating and drinking. Her chubby frame had been peeled down so that you could see the bones in her fingers, feel how tight the skin was around her wrists, notice the paleness of her feet. Her skin was burning, and in certain spots it was as if large, razor-sharp needles were being pressed slowly into her flesh. She wished that she would die. Instead, she was sent to England.

At finishing school she was put under the direct supervision of an ancient but merciless woman named Madame Yuplait. Madame Yuplait had once been a courtesan. She was skilled with a whip and for a time became quite famous for snapping buttons off the waistcoats of men at parties. When she lost her looks, she changed her name, moved to London, opened Madame Yuplait's Finishing School for Young Ladies, and quickly developed a reputation for turning troubled girls into debutantes.

Miss Waldron did not slap the maid when she arrived with her steamer trunk, but she refused to tip the driver. The man caused such a scene that Madame Yuplait had to pay him herself. For this embarrassment Miss Waldron was sent to the attic.

The attic bedrooms could only be locked from the outside. They were the hottest rooms in the summer and the coldest in the winter. The walls were orange and the ceilings red. Girls were sent there to be broken.

At Madame Yuplait's Finishing School for Young Ladies, Miss Waldron became acquainted with which fork to use, the mysteries of the corset, and the proper way to enter a room. She learned how to arrange flowers, how to play the harp, how to keep her stomach from making embarrassing noises in public. She was taught how to smile through pain, how to turn her head into the light, how to lay her hand on a table. She practiced the intonation of certain words and phrases in French, German, Spanish, Arabic, Swedish, and Italian, as well as proper English, because Madame said her accent was abominable.

Miss Waldron came close to asking her father for help. She wrote him a plaintive letter full of promises and regrets, but she never mailed it.

She tried to think of other people who might come to her aid. The other students respected her wildness and enjoyed gossiping about her adventures, but few would cross the line and call her their friend. Miss Waldron considered her voice instructor, her makeup instructor, her poise instructor. Then she remembered the Italian.

She found Maria and Fredo living together in a small Soho flat, both having renounced their inheritances. Maria now tended her hair herself. It was full of split ends. She kept a tiny pair of scissors on a ribbon around her neck, and whenever there was a lull in the conversation, she would begin individually clipping the ragged strands. Fredo drew pictures of tourists on the street. At night they made love so loudly the neighbors called the police.

Miss Waldron began to visit them on Saturdays after confession. Together they would go to the local saloons and drink until early evening. No one at the finishing school questioned these long absences at first. But Miss Waldron's father had his private detectives and Madame had her intuition, so it was not long before the group was discovered and flushed out.

Ten lashes were given to Miss Waldron's soft white behind, as well as two weeks of nothing but oatmeal. But it was too late. The damage had already been done, for on one sunny afternoon, at a heavy round wooden table in the Brightenshead Tavern, Fredo had introduced Miss Waldron to the great white hunter Mister Willoughby Lowe.

He was not what she expected. Miss Waldron had seen movies of hunters—*Tarzan* and *King Kong*—and they wore jodhpurs and white pith helmets and were always clean-shaven and had clefts in their chins. Willoughby Lowe had a square head, small red lips like a woman's, a thick beard that covered most of his face, and only one ear. The other had been blown off while he was shooting crocodiles in South America.

I'm lucky, he said. *The guide lost a leg. I just passed out and learned to say, Eh?* He cocked his head at Miss Waldron and looked at her curiously, as though she'd just said something important he'd missed.

His face seemed older than his body. She noticed fine lines carving their way into his cheeks, across his forehead, and stamping rings around his eyes. She could see where his skin would crease if he chose to smile.

The more Miss Waldron looked at Willoughby Lowe, the more she began to think of meat—round steak, T-bones, filet mignon—red, cool, thick flesh marbled over onto itself. His shoulders were hulking and his back was curved with muscle—thick slabs on either side of his spine like a well-toned side of beef.

He pushed up his sleeve to show them a tattoo of a spiral he'd received as an initiation rite from a tribe in Papua New Guinea. She could see the veins in his arm popped and sprouting like rivers of blue, coursing and connecting just below his skin. She closed her eyes for a moment and thought of running her fingers along those veins, reading them like Braille, and imagined the experience would be like singing.

Later, she discovered that underneath his clothes he was covered with hair. It coursed down his neck, across his chest, and onto his shoulders, fanned over his back, swirled onto his legs, and concentrated in a thick dark forest between his thighs. The only place he was hairless was on his behind.

Like a baboon, Willoughby said.

The hair frightened her at first. She did not know where to put her hands. It was coarse and curled and smelled slightly earthy, like a pile of fallen leaves. He bristled as he pressed against her, and the difference between their bodies made Miss Waldron feel suddenly tiny and weak, like a hairless newborn. She dug her fingers into his fur and clung to him.

Everything changed when he started to sweat. A glistening sheen came over his body and he began to glow. He buried his face in her neck, and the hair softened and flattened out until it felt like feathers, as if she were being stroked with tiny silken brushes. She was covered with a slick wetness. Her hands slid from his neck, from his shoulders, from his back, from everything she tried to hold on to.

Later as she stood before the washbasin in the corner of the room, she saw that she was covered with his hair. Tiny black, curling strands stuck to the film of sweat still hovering across her breasts and stomach. She drew a finger from one nipple to the other and left behind a clear trail, as if she were shaving.

Look! she said, spinning around, but Willoughby Lowe was already snoring away.

Madame Yuplait could tell what had happened. Miss Waldron was glowing like a firecracker, and there was an arch in her back that had not been there before. Madame beat her ferociously. Miss Waldron gripped the sides of the bed, bit her lips, and tried to hold still.

The private detectives also knew. They had followed Miss Waldron to Willoughby Lowe's hotel, watched her making love through the keyhole, sucked in their breath as she drew her finger across her breasts, and regarded her over the tops of newspapers as she whisked through the lobby.

They had grown fond of Miss Waldron over the years. They had watched her develop from a spindly child to a woman with serious character. There were times when they thought of her as their own daughter, biting their nails as she climbed out of windows, hitchhiked down highways, and learned how to drink whiskey. But they were silent parents, like ghosts, only witnesses. They were never able to tell her no, to say stop, to give her warning, or to stroke her head while she was sleeping. They laid fingertips on her bony elbow as they returned her to her keepers, and tried hard to find ways from caring too much.

Sometimes the private detectives wondered if Miss Waldron knew they were there, recording every minute of her outside world. There were moments—a hesitant smile, a glance into the darkness before she slipped through a door—that said she did. At least this is what they secretly hoped—that sometimes she was doing what she was doing simply to give them something exciting to watch.

So when they saw Miss Waldron on the roof of the finishing school with a hatbox in her hand, the private detectives exchanged knowing hand signals. Before long a ladder slid across from one of the neighboring buildings, and, after steadying it, Miss Waldron crawled across the open space— six stories high—the handle of the hatbox in her teeth, her dress hitched around her waist, and her silk panties flashing for all the world to see.

The detectives dispatched a telegram to Miss Waldron's father: *DAUGHTER HAS ESCAPED FROM MADAME YUPLAIT STOP ON HER WAY TO GHANA STOP APPEARS TO BE IN LOVE STOP INSTRUCTIONS?*

They received no reply.

On the steamship to Africa, Miss Waldron posed as Willoughby Lowe's personal secretary. This did not fool anyone. At night their moans and lovers' curses could be heard throughout the ship, vibrating along the edges of the steel hull, echoing back and forth into the furnace of the coal room, singing out across the waves like whale songs from the propeller. The expedition team scientists tossed and turned in their cabins, and the crew groaned down in their bunks.

When they arrived, Miss Waldron realized that everything in Africa was covered with dust. The roads, the animals, even the people. Willoughby told her they used it to ward off flies. Miss Waldron saw the point, and quickly traded her dresses for native clothes—soft layers of light woven cotton. Her high-heeled shoes were used to bargain with the porters, and she slipped into a pair of Willoughby's boots.

The scientists had arranged for everything in advance. As they divided their boxes of sample test tubes and books on species identification between the porters, a guide appeared. Willoughby seemed to know him, and after a friendly exchange of greetings, he whispered to Miss Waldron that the man was a slave. Once they were in the jungle, the slave coordinated everything—where the tents should go, how the food should be stored, and when to start the fire. As darkness came and they sat around the flames, Miss Waldron listened to the sounds of the forest and studied him.

It seemed as though his skin had been peeled off in strips. She found it hard to distinguish his nostrils among the lines of pink and brown and black— bubbly sections of destroyed muscle and scar tissue crisscrossed his body like worms. Despite this she could see underneath that he was strong, about thirty years old. His eyes were large and bright, and she noticed that when he closed them, the lids disappeared into the tangle of his face.

He did not sleep with the rest of them. Once the team had retired, the slave climbed a tree and tied a hammock among the branches. From there he kept watch over the fire. He had a machete beside him to kill the snakes and a shotgun to frighten poachers.

In the morning Miss Waldron watched Willoughby Lowe unpack his guns. She asked about the slave's face and was told he'd been locked in an oven. His master had caught him trying to escape, and by the time he was dragged out from the cinders, most of his skin was gone. The slave was brought back to life by a witch doctor and later sold to one of the directors of the Natural History Museum, who used him as a point man for the African expeditions.

Why don't you release him? Miss Waldron asked.

He's got a much better life with us, said Willoughby.

After a breakfast of bacon, the group headed off into the jungle with a jar of water and a rack of loaded weapons. The slave led the way. Miss Waldron carried a slender pistol in her back pocket and kept her eyes on the canopy. They were looking for monkeys.

Willoughby shot a chimpanzee and three baboons, then announced that it was time for tea—biscuits from a can and a weak English breakfast. Miss Waldron wandered over to the carcasses of the animals with her cup and saucer. She had watched them drop from the trees. The guns exploded and the monkeys fell like fruit, whipping through the leaves, breaking through branches, rolling down to thuds in the dirt. The screeching and the rustling that followed as the other animals fled the area was unnerving. She had not realized how many had been so near.

Miss Waldron reached out a finger and touched the wrinkled nose of a dead baboon. Its mouth was open, its tongue bloody through sharp incisors, but its eyes were closed in a sweet way, as though it were sleeping. She glanced around, then leaned forward and kissed it.

The private detectives snapped the picture and sent it airmail to Miss Waldron's father. They had spent the day sweating, hacking through the jungle with machetes, spraying themselves with bug repellent, and dodging wild boars. Their cigarettes were damp. They watched Miss Waldron through their binoculars and tried to keep a low profile. They began to wonder if there wasn't easier work.

Meanwhile, Miss Waldron learned to climb trees. For days she had been watching the slave wrap his bare feet against bark and propel himself into the canopy. It reminded her of the days she had spent in the circus, and in the early morning she would practice, shimmying up the trunk. Before long she made it a foot off the ground, then two, then three. She began spending her afternoon siesta in a low-slung hammock, which rose each day among the vines along with her ability.

At dusk Willoughby would go looking for her. There'd been a change in Miss Waldron since they moved into the forest, but Willoughby was used to seeing people go native. He'd done it himself, once or twice. As the porters prepared meals, Willoughby would rouse her by calling out the courses. PLUM PUDDING WITH RRRRUM SAUCE! he would shout into the bush. CHA-TEAUBRIAND SIMMERED IN WINE! Sooner or later he would hear leaves rustling, and then the soft thud of her small feet hitting the ground.

Miss Waldron brought a rifle. She'd been prac-ticing with heavier guns, firing at empty biscuit cans and melons. She moved through the jungle next to Willoughby, and this time when she felt him sight a monkey, she was not shaken by the shot or the sounds of the other animals fleeing. She drew near as the men tied the creature's arms and legs together and slid it on a stick for carrying.

The monkey had been shot once through the stomach. What remained of the coat shimmered and bristled, a combination of reds. The long, thin fingers curled tightly into themselves, holding on to nothing. Its face was a tight black mask. Miss Waldron reached down and touched the tail, and the monkey turned and sank its teeth into her arm.

In one movement the slave raised his machete and sliced through the animal's neck, so that when Miss Waldron pulled her arm away, the head came with it.

It's a colobus, said Willoughby. *I've never seen one like this before.* He pushed his fingers into the nose, eased the jaw back, and delicately took the monkey's head from Miss Waldron's arm as if he were removing a bracelet.

That night the scientists broke open the whiskey. They had spent all day taking the colobus apart and had decided that it was an entirely new species. Willoughby promised the scientists that he would shoot ten more. He promised Miss Waldron that he would name it after her.

They sat around the fire and told bawdy stories, and when they were very drunk they danced. They did waltzes and two-steps, minuets and the Charleston, all to the sound of flutes carved out of gourds. Willoughby shook his rump. Miss Waldron did the cancan. The men shot their guns in the air and then passed out, one by one.

The private detectives waited patiently nearby in a grove of cacao trees. They had received one line from Miss Waldron's father: *RETURN MONKEY GIRL TO BE FINISHED.*

The detectives lingered until they could hear Willoughby Lowe snoring. The moon shone silver as they stepped over the sleeping scientists. Miss Waldron's feet were hanging out of the tent. In the glow they looked half-alive, like fish freshly killed. The private detectives held above the ankles and silently yanked the rest of her out.

Miss Waldron was dreaming. She was in a hospital bed, and the sheets were binding her legs. There were monkey skulls holding her wrists. She could hear the footsteps of her father approaching. Above her were tangled roots with eyes. The slave leaned forward and told her to wake up. When she did she found herself being carried over the heads of the detectives into the jungle.

It was as if she were sinking. The moonlight flickered through the leaves like waves. She could hear the *shlop shlop* of her kidnappers' shoes as they hurried through the mud. A veil of moss passed over her face. It tasted like cobwebs. She sensed a weight in her stomach where her father had kicked her, knotted like a stone.

The teeth marks on her arm began to scream. Miss Waldron heard them and started to fight. She struggled and flailed and punched and bit. She was a full-grown woman now, and it took all the strength of the three detectives to keep possession of her.

There were shadows overhead. She knew that somewhere in them there were limbs to hang on to. Miss Waldron stretched, hoping to catch a branch. She imagined the trees reaching back for her. Long arms giving chase through the darkness. Her fingertips touched bark, touched fur, touched skin. Then she felt something take hold of her hands and she was lifted into the canopy.

Miss Waldron was missing. So was the slave. Willoughby Lowe searched the jungle, tearing through creepers, behind every bush, underneath every gathering of leaves. He was inconsolable. The scientists were convinced the monkey bite had made Miss Waldron mad.

For several weeks the private detectives staked out Willoughby's camp, hoping to catch her again. They trailed the expedition's search party and even learned to climb trees, boosting each other on their shoulders and clinging to vines. They dusted the forest for fingerprints. They hunted all day and into the night until finally, nervous, they informed her father of the escape. The detectives received an immediate reply: *NO MORE BANANAS STOP YOU ARE FIRED*.

They decided to continue the search.

The private detectives contacted other private detectives. They called on spies; they called in favors. They got in touch with infiltrators and double agents, bounty hunters and Boy Scouts, anyone who might see something and report it. They cast their nets wide and waited.

They got a tip. Miss Waldron had been seen on a camel, going toward Egypt. The detectives donned their fedoras and headed out of the jungle, but when they reached the desert, her trail had turned to dust. A few weeks later Miss Waldron was sighted near a Hindu temple in Kashmir. A month afterward she was in Papua New Guinea. Six months passed and she was sledding through the Yukon, wrapped in furs, urging her team of dogs on with a smile and an occasional kick of the boot.

The detectives missed her. They kept missing her. Years passed and they grew weary of traveling without a destination. Eventually they moved back to Minnesota and became security guards. They read about her colobus in zoological textbooks and issues of *Primate Monthly*. Sometimes they would hear from an old contact—a Miss Waldron had been heard, a Miss Waldron had been smelled, a Miss Waldron had been spotted in the trees. These sightings grew fewer and farther between, and then they stopped completely.

A NOTE TO THE READER

about "Miss Waldron's Red Colobus":

Native to Ghana and the Ivory Coast, Miss Waldron's Red Colobus (*Procolobus badius Waldroni*) was first described by scientists in 1936, based on eight specimens shot in 1933 by a man named Willoughby P. Lowe, a collector for British Museums. Lowe named the monkey "Miss Waldron" for one Miss F. Waldron, who was described in records simply as Mr. Lowe's "traveling companion." The monkey was declared extinct in 2000, but in 2002 the freshly cut skin of a Miss Waldron's Red Colobus was discovered, raising hopes that the animal still exists.

Although loosely based on historical fact, all characters and events in this story are fictional.

ACKNOWLEDGMENTS

There are many people who have helped bring this collection to life. My readers, fellow writers and loyal friends: Helen Ellis and Ann Napolitano. My magic-working agent: Nicole Aragi. My brilliant editor: Susan Kamil. The best assistants in publishing: Margo Lipschultz, Alissa Shipp and Tenette Ludlow. My teachers: Blanche Boyd, Barbara Jones, Paule Marshall, Dani Shapiro, A. M. Homes and E. L. Doctorow. Organizations that provided time and places to write: New York University's Graduate Creative Writing Program, Hedgebrook, The Writers Room, Blue Mountain Center and the New York State Writers Institute's Master Writer Mentoring Program. Editors who gave me boosts along the way: Lois Rosenthal, Will Allison, Anne Brashler, Marie Hayes, Robin Lauzon, Ronald Spatz, Nicholas Delbanco, Sydney Lea, Michael Koch, Otto Penzler and Michael Connelly. Forgiving employers who hired me for "real jobs": Writers House, Jennifer Lyons, Gordon Pattee, Alex Steele, and Howard Stringer and the Stringettes: Virginia Garity, Barbara Benesch and Suzie Nash. Friends who offered advice and encouragement: Maribeth Batcha, Ariane Fink, Kate Gray, John Hodgman, Yuka Lawrence, Karin Schulze and especially Alex Twersky for his love and support. My sisters, who make me laugh harder than anything: Honorah Tinti and Hester Tinti-Kane. And finally my parents: Hester and William Tinti, patient listeners of my dreams.

ABOUT THE AUTHOR

HANNAH TINTI grew up in Salem, Massachusetts. Her work has appeared in *Best American Mystery Stories, Story Quarterly*, and *Epoch*, among other publications. She is currently the editor of *One Story* magazine.

27.95

16X - FC
17X - FC
20X - FC